OVER THE TOP

ALISON HUGHES

RP|KIDS
PHILADELPHIA

Running Press Kids
Hachette Book Group
1290 Avenue of the Americas, New York, NY 10104
www.runningpress.com/rpkids
@RP_Kids

Printed in the United States of America

First Edition: August 2021

Published by Running Press Kids, an imprint of Perseus Books, LLC, a subsidiary of Hachette Book Group, Inc. The Running Press Kids name and logo is a trademark of the Hachette Book Group.

The Hachette Speakers Bureau provides a wide range of authors for speaking events. To find out more, go to www.hachettespeakersbureau.com or call (866) 376-6591.

The publisher is not responsible for websites (or their content) that are not owned by the publisher.

Print book cover and interior design by Frances J. Soo Ping Chow.

Library of Congress Cataloging-in-Publication Data
Names: Hughes, Alison, 1966-author. Title: Over the top / Alison Hughes. Description: First edition. | New York, NY : Running Press Kids, 2021. Identifiers: LCCN 2020046319 | ISBN 9780762473120 (hardcover) | ISBN 9780762473137 (ebook) Subjects: CYAC: Family life—Fiction. | Middle schools—Fiction. | Schools—Fiction. | Parties—Fiction. | Theater—Fiction. | Moving, Household—Fiction. Classification: LCC PZ7.H8731144 Ove 2021 | DDC [Fic]—dc23 LC record available at https://lccn.loc.gov/2020046319

ISBNs: 978-0-7624-7312-0 (hardcover), 978-0-7624-7313-7 (ebook)

LSC-C

Printing 1, 2021

For My Family

CHAPTER 1

The Show-Stopper, Jaw-Dropper, Very Last House

There was no getting away from it: the house was pink. It wasn't a shade of coral or peach. It wasn't pink-*ish*. It was vivid, candy-floss, lip-gloss pink. Bright pink. *Deliberately* pink. In-your-face pink.

That can't be the house we're thinking of actually living in. Oh, please no. That cannot be it.

I swiveled around, searching up and down the pretty, tree-lined street. The only "For Sale" sign was in front of the enormous pink house. This was it.

Dad slid our new van to a stop under a tree by the long drive-way. There was a moment of silence as he cut the engine and the four of us looked out the windows. The house glowed through the trees like a giant, princess-themed bouncy castle.

Because not only was it pink, it was also a sort-of castle. Two towers with pointed roofs poked up from the back of the house to frame the triple-car garage, and four enormous pillars held up a large, pink triangle above the floor-to-ceiling windows. There were massive, wooden, "none shall pass!" double front doors.

"Ridiculous," I muttered, crossing my arms and shaking my head. This house was supposed to be the best of the bunch. The realtor had promised us that the last house we were to look at was the most special house on her list. The show-stopper.

"What're those . . . ? Ah, turrets," said Dad, looking down at the paper the realtor had given us. "Built in 1993, though . . ."

"A good year for *moats*," I said sarcastically. "Wait, *is* there a moat?" I wouldn't have put it past the owners of this house to have gone full-castle and built a moat with a drawbridge somewhere. A pink drawbridge.

"Wow!" laughed Hero, bouncing in his seat. "A solid pink house! *Weird!* Let's look!" My nine-year-old brother scrambled out of his seat and hauled open the van door.

"I love it," breathed Mom, giving Dad one of her painful, excited little arm squeezes. "*A-dore* it! It's perfect. I don't even think I need to look inside!" My dad gave her an amused look. "Oh, maybe just a peek." She slipped out of the van and shrieked and waved at the realtor, who had just pulled into the driveway.

"Erica! Erica! You *angel*! How did you *find* this place?"

How did she *find* it, Mom? You could probably see this house from outer space.

Dad turned to look back at me and raised his eyebrows. "Well, Diva? What do you think?"

"Are you *serious*, Dad? Look at it. Will you *look* at this house? It's ridiculous. Tacky! Like, beyond tacky. There's not even a word for it. Do *you* want to live in Disneyland? Is that what you had in mind?"

Dad raised both hands and shrugged his shoulders. "Okay, okay, let's not make up our minds before we've even seen the inside. Keep an open mind. Great neighborhood, great school right down the street, *really* good price for the square footage."

"It's cheap because—"

"Hey, I didn't say *cheap.*"

"—because nobody wants to live in a pink fake castle, Dad! Other than the people who built it, I guess. And Mom. And possibly—" I floundered for a few seconds "—circus people!"

Dad sighed. "Backs onto the river, which might be nice. Private. Nature. Come on, Deev, let's at least take a look."

We walked up the long driveway, pausing at a huge, bronze-colored statue of a centaur in full horse-trot. The human part of the creature waved an enormous, rippling bronze flag, which had the house number engraved on it.

"Daaad," I wailed, holding out both my hands, presenting the statue to him. "Seriously? This? I actually have no words for this. Why this? A *centaur*? Why not a *knight*, if you're going for a castle theme? Or a dragon. I mean, obviously, why a statue at *all*, but what is this even trying to *say*?"

Dad was studying the sheet in his hand.

"Yep, centaur comes with it. Jeez, says it's *nine feet tall*!" Dad looked up at the centaur with new respect. "That puppy'd have set them back a bit, I bet."

"Again, *why*?"

Hero came running to meet us. "Oh, good, you saw the horse-guy."

"Pretty hard to miss," I said.

"Isn't he *cool*?" He paused to gasp in a breath. "I'll call him Gary if we get the house."

Gary the Centaur. Why not? I stifled a hysterical giggle.

"Why Gary?" Dad asked.

"He just looks like a Gary," Hero said. "You know. Just: Gary. Suits him. Could I climb up and *ride* this guy, Dad?"

"Better not just yet," smiled Dad. "But if we buy the place, off you go, cowboy! Gary will be your trusty steed. Let's go have a look."

"C'mon, there are some *huge* trees around back. Great for climbing. And a spikey fence. Don't climb that. It hurts. And the river is right past the fence, and there's also a little kind of *house* right in the middle of the backyard!"

"Garden gazebo," Dad said, looking at the paper. "Sounds nice."

"Is it pink, too, 'Ro?" I asked dully.

"Sort of. Actually, maybe more purplish."

I closed my eyes.

Dad put an arm around my shoulders and pulled me to the front door.

"Courage, Diva," he said. "Be brave."

"Pink overload," I said, pretend-staggering. "So much pink. The glare. My eyes, my eyes . . ."

Dad laughed, which cheered me up a little. He didn't look so pale and tired when he laughed.

"Ever heard of *paint*, Diva? Comes in lots of colors. The pink doesn't have to be forever. C'mon, 'Ro, let's show Diva around the place."

There were huge, iron lion's-head door knockers attached to each massive door. Dad grabbed one by its gaping, fanging jaw and swung it experimentally. *Thunk-thunk.*

"Heavy," he said.

"And pointless," I said, indicating the doorbell.

"Let's just go *inside* already," said Hero, pushing open the door.

"Empty!" said Hero with satisfaction, kicking off his shoes. "I *love* the empty ones!" He sprinted a lap of the massive entryway, performed two awkward cartwheels, and took off down a hallway.

"Diva! Deeee-va!" Mom was calling urgently from somewhere deep inside the house, her voice muffled by the wall-to-wall pink carpet. I looked at Dad.

"Where—?"

Dad tilted his head, listening.

"I think . . . maybe thataway," he said, pointing me down a long hall off to the right.

I eventually found Mom in the family room off the kitchen. She was standing over by the window, a billowy curtain clutched in her hand, her other hand over her mouth.

"Deeeee-va! Oh, there you are. What took you so long?"

"I didn't know where—"

"Quick, come here! Come *right this minute!*"

I ran over, glancing at Erica the realtor, who was talking on her cellphone several blocks away in the kitchen. "Are you okay, Mom? What—?"

"Look at how *beautiful* that is," Mom interrupted, putting her arm around my shoulders. "Isn't it beautiful? I thought you should see this. You're the writer. You appreciate atmosphere. *Setting.* See how the lawn leads into those gorgeous trees—" her hand waved gracefully "—and then it slopes right down to the river?" She squealed. "It's just so, so . . ."

"Beautiful?" Mom pretended not to notice my flat voice. I felt a little bit guilty. Because the view *was* beautiful, it really was. But Mom always made such a big deal of everything, that my reflex was always to make it smaller. And then I'd feel guilty, because she was genuinely enthusiastic about almost everything. Which was, once again, annoying. Vicious cycle.

"Yes!" Mom sighed, clasping her hands theatrically under her chin. "Oh, I have a great feeling about this house, Princess! A really, really, super-great feeling."

My heart sank. Whenever Mom had "a great feeling" or a "great idea" about something, it meant trouble. The day-to-day hassles associated with "nice vibes," "good karma," or even "hinkies" I could deal with. But "great feelings" were booming warning bells.

Dad wandered into the room.

"Great basement. Lots of room, lots of storage. Hey, nice view here," he said.

"Nice!" Mom shrieked in protest, punching his shoulder playfully. "'Nice,' he says! Understatement of the *century*! It's glorious! It's *magical*! Right on the river like that . . ."

"Hmm, could be damp," murmured Dad, peering out. "Wonder what that might do to the house's foundation?"

". . . and so private with all those lovely trees! And such a great neighborhood. Top of the line. Erica there"—Mom gestured over at the realtor—"tells me that the schools down the street are the best in the city. The best! In the whole city! Right down the street from our house!"

I saw Dad look down at Mom's radiant face, and his own face softened. He smiled at her and she slipped her hand into his.

I looked away. There should be a word, I thought, for the cringey feeling kids get when they see their parents cuddling in any way. It's a feeling similar to, but not the same as, the feeling they get when they see their parents (or any adults) dancing.

I'll have to remember those two feelings to add to my book, I thought.

My newest writing project was my biggest one yet: I was writing a dictionary of new words to describe commonly felt thoughts and feelings that have no word for them. At least in English. Like, for example, the feeling you might get when your family is about to buy a house that is so embarrassing that "tacky" or "ridiculous" doesn't even begin to describe it.

My language arts teacher at my old school gave me the idea. When school ended last fall, I said there should be a word for the feeling of the last day of school.

"You know, sort of a happy feeling, but sad, too, where everything's packed up and the class looks different and the windows are open because it's almost summer and there's that smell of dry weeds and cut grass and there aren't any rules, and things are changing . . ."

Mrs. Katamba had listened, smiling, leaning her tired face on her hand.

"You have a real gift for words, Diva. I know exactly what you mean. Well, there's your new writing project! Coming up with words for those situations or feelings we all recognize, we all *know*, but can't express."

"That's way too big a project," I said. "That'd be basically a dictionary. I don't think I could do it, Mrs. Katamba. I can't even think of a word for that feeling I just described."

"Well, don't worry about that now. Think of the feelings first," Mrs. Katamba said. "Write the *feelings*. The words can come later."

It was an amazing idea. Because I've often thought there should a word for things like that weird feeling you get in your stomach when the bus beside your bus moves, and you thought it was *your bus* that was moving but it wasn't. Or a word for that feeling when a friend's lunch looks way more delicious than yours does. Or a word for that feeling of being free and semi-important and alone in the school halls if you get picked to take something down to the office. Or for that panicked pause where something on the floor *might* be a gigantic bug, but it turns out to be a snarl of hair or something. Or for that helpless, uncertain feeling when you should be telling your friend they have food on their face, but you don't want to embarrass them, and then it's gone on too long and . . .

The more I thought about it, the more potential words there were. My feelings list just kept growing. It was already March, and I was still discovering all the feelings. The words would come later.

I turned away from my hand-holding parents and wandered into the kitchen. It even had countertops of pale-pink stone. These people were absolute monsters for the pink. They must have gone on some pink-themed shopping spree, buying every single pink thing in the city, leaving other pink-loving people to grudgingly buy other colors. Where do you even find pale-pink stone? I ran my hand down the cool, smooth surface.

The feeling of wandering in a giant, empty house, I thought. *The feeling of missing your old, cramped house, your old school, your old friends, the way things used to be.*

Mom bustled over to me, her round face smiling.

"Let's go and check out our bedrooms, Princess!" she said, pulling me over to a sweeping staircase.

CHAPTER 2

Turret Bedrooms and Massive, Unwanted Mirrors

We climbed the stairs, the plush carpet muffling our footsteps.

"Not sure about all this pink, Rosie," Dad said, looking down at the carpet. "No pun intended."

Mom giggled.

"It *does* suit my name, doesn't it? Rosie in a pink house. Like it was meant to be! Anyway, the carpet isn't *pink*, Mike. It's *champagne*. Just a whisper of pink. Perfect for a *prin-cess*." She sang that last word and twirled around to wink at me.

"Whoa! Whoa, there, princess," I said, bracing myself on the railing and putting out a hand to steady her. "Let's just get you up this endless staircase without you breaking your royal leg or something."

A wall of mirrors met us at the top of the staircase. Floor to ceiling, wall to wall.

Not good. I sneaked a look at my reflection, then looked away. This little princess is not looking so good.

That feeling of always seeming to notice yourself in a mirror and then wishing you hadn't because you look much worse than you ever thought you did. Another one to add to the list.

I imagined having to face my full-length reflection every single time I ran up or down these stairs. To have to look, in full-length detail, at my thin, gangly body, my oddly freckled face with those wicked purple smudges under my eyes that never went away no matter how much I slept. To constantly see the frizzy dark curls escaping from my ponytail every single time I went to and from my room. I looked away from the mirror. This pink house was diabolical.

Mom stopped and posed in front of the mirror, running a hand through her thick, curly, shoulder-length black hair.

"Well who are *those* gorgeous folks?" she laughed, wiggling her plump fingers in a little wave at the mirror. "Especially this one! This gorgeous girl here!" Mom spun me to face the mirror.

I stood awkwardly, expressionless, with Mom's smiling, dancing face by my shoulder.

I don't believe you anymore, Mom. I am not gorgeous. I have never been gorgeous. I never will be. I am a plain, odd mixture of your short, chubby Indian-ness and Dad's tall, skinny white-ness. I am not brown or white, I am not "lovely butterscotch" or "delicious caramel" as you always say. Hero is. I am just a washed-out beige.

My hazel eyes met my mom's sparkling brown ones in the mirror.

"Yeah, all those supermodels better look out, Mom," I said, wriggling away from her hands. "Can we just look at this stupid house now, please?" I saw her smile fade as I stalked away down the hall.

"Diva!" Hero's voice called from somewhere at the far end of the hallway. "Deev, down here!"

I went down the hall and opened a door on the right. Closet. *Huge* closet, shelves running side to side. Bedroom-sized closet. The door farther down on the left was a dark bedroom (he wouldn't be in there. 'Ro hated the dark).

"Keep calling, 'Ro!" I yelled. "I'm trying to find you."

"Here!"

Another door. Nope: bathroom. *Big* bathroom. Bigger than my old bedroom. Bigger, I think, than our old living room. Two sinks. Massive, centaur-sized bathtub.

"Keep calling!" I stifled a giggle. This was so stupid. If we bought this house, were we going to go through this hide-and-seek routine every time we wanted to talk to each other?

"Here!"

"Where the heck—?" Another dark room.

"Here!"

I finally reached the last door at the end of the hall, and there he was.

"There you are. *Finally*," he said. He spread his short arms wide. "What do you think of my amazing room?"

"Oh, *your* room, huh?" I said. "You sound just like Mom." Not only did 'Ro sound like Mom, he looked like her, as well. He *was* like her. Jet-black, thick wavy hair, liquid brown eyes, a face that crumpled easily into a big smile, a sunny, happy personality.

I walked into the room and looked around. And around. And around. It was a circular room, one of the turret rooms. Hero was right: it *was* amazing.

Light streamed in from four high windows, and from the two tall, regular windows overlooking the backyard and the river. Hero looked very small sitting and dangling his legs from a wide bench built underneath the window.

"Wow," I said, "this is actually a pretty cool room. Very . . . round." I turned in another circle, trying to imagine where on earth you would put a bed. Right in the center? That seemed weird. Beds should have a side, maybe two sides, touching a wall, shouldn't they? Some completely immature part of me thought that otherwise you would be surrounded by potential monsters and various creepy-crawlies on all *four* sides, instead of only two sides. But I wasn't going to mention that to 'Ro.

"Yeah," Hero said excitedly, his face flushed, "imagine this seat thing piled with pillows and a quilt! You could read forever in here! Plus"—he pointed up—"those windows don't have any curtains, so it would almost always be light in here. *Plus*, you could leave a light on. What are you doing?"

I'd dropped to the floor and was lying on my back in the middle of the room.

"I'm trying to imagine what it would be like to have a bed right in the middle like this. Weird."

"There's another room like this for you," Hero said slowly. "But it's way on the other side of the house. Really far away, actually, even if you ran fast. It's all the way down this long hall, past the staircase, then down the next hall. At the end." He looked anxious. In our old house, our tiny bedrooms had been right beside each other, within calling-when-it-was-scary-dark distance, within knocking-on-the-wall reach. "It would take a while for me to get over there if you were scared at night or something," he said, swallowing.

Riiight. If *I* were scared, tough guy.

"Hey, you're right, 'Ro. Thanks for thinking of that," I said. He tried to hide the relief in his face by nodding matter-of-factly. "But actually, I'm not crazy about having one of these turret rooms," I assured him. "I mean, I like it, it's very 'you.' But I'm more of a square-room person. Rectangular. Corners-girl. If we even get this house. Which we might not."

"Mom loves it." Hero said. We looked at each other. We both knew the force of Mom's enthusiasm.

I sighed. 'Ro was right. Mom had a "great feeling" about this house. A "super-great" feeling. We would all get swept along in Mom's huge plans, like we always did. We were almost certainly going to live in this ridiculous, enormous pink house.

"I think there's a bedroom next door to this one," Hero said. "Looked nice. C'mon, let's check it out."

When we pulled open the curtains, the dark bedroom next door sprang to life. It was probably four times the size of my old room, but in this house, it seemed cozy.

"Square, just like you like 'em," Hero said, trying to sell it to me. "And look! Another window seat where you could write *and* a whole wall of shelves already built in there for all your books!" He knocked his knuckles against them. "Solid wood."

"A definite maybe," I said. I'd always loved the idea of having lots of shelves. In my old room, my books had been stacked in teetering piles everywhere, leaving only a little aisle for walking from the door to the bed. I hadn't really minded. I still knew where everything was.

The feeling of preferring somewhere cramped and inconvenient to a place that is, according to most people, clearly way better. I made a mental note of that one. But was it only me who felt like that?

Out in the hall, the realtor was leading Mom and Dad down to the master bedroom, several miles down the hallway.

". . . and with the ensuite bathroom, *this* is the third full bath. Double sink. Jetted tub. Italian tile. Heated floors. Heated towel racks."

"Gorgeous. Just gorgeous," marveled Mom.

"Hey, you two," Dad perked up when he saw us. "I'll catch up with you in a sec, Rosie. Okay, Erica?"

"Sure thing, Mike." Erica smiled briefly and automatically at us.

When they were gone, Dad turned to us.

"Big place, huh? So, completely honestly, what do you think, guys? What's your gut say?"

"I like it," said 'Ro. "I mean, it's the best house we've seen *by far*. It's huge, and the trees are *great* . . ." He trailed off uncertainly, then perked up. "I've picked out my room! So has Deev!"

"Not really. Not for keeps," I said quickly.

"Hey, great! The turret rooms?"

"Yeah, about that, Dad," I said. "Turrets? A castle? I'm not even mentioning the pink. I've moved on from the pink. Blocked it out. But there are only four of us. Four people. Why are we looking at this house that could sleep a small city?"

Dad sighed and ran a hand through his thinning hair. He looked at me with tired hazel eyes.

"You know, Deev, Mom and I always said that when the time was right, we'd move to some place really wonderful. A dream house! You know that neither of us had much growing up. We've saved and saved our whole lives, and now the construction company's business is booming. Absolutely booming! And Mom's going to expand her party-planning business as well. We need some *space* for everything. Remember the basement in our old house?"

Our basement had been a sea of stacked boxes and totes. But it hadn't been just the basement that had been totally taken over by Mom's business. Decorations had been stuffed in every cupboard and closet, bins of plastic flowers stacked behind the television, ribbons and party favors had spilled out from under beds, bunches of balloons had bobbed above the kitchen table.

"We can finally afford something big, something with a lot of space, where I can have a home office, Mom can have workspace and storage, where you kids can have lots of friends over, where we'll have room to grow. Something great, something over the top! Why not? Look how much fun your mom's having with this house!"

I glanced over the bannister, and a rueful smile tugged at my mouth. Mom was singing and forcibly waltzing an awkward Erica around the living room. *That's how I must look when Mom does that to me*, I thought, watching Erica's stiff, staggering, off-balance steps as she clutched her clipboard. Better save the poor lady.

"Mom!" I called, "maybe you should come up here for a family conference?"

"Sure thing, Princess!" Mom released Erica, who looked

up with relief. Mom puffed up the stairs. "Whoo, *lots* of stairs! Okay, Rosie has finally arrived! Serious stuff: family conference," she said, looking at our faces, sliding an arm around 'Ro.

"We need to know how everyone's feeling about the house," Dad said, looking at me. "We'll want to see the rest—"

"I've seen it all. It's gorgeous," said Mom.

"And the yard."

"Beautiful."

"And we'll have to get it inspected, of course, but I guess we need to know whether it's a yes or a no for everyone."

"YES," said Mom, crossing the fingers on both hands and looking at us pleadingly. "It's my dream house! But it depends on you and the kids, too, of course."

"Yep," said Hero. "Of all the ones we've seen, this one's the best."

"Diva?" asked Dad.

"No, you first. What do *you* say, Dad?"

"Compared with the others we've looked at, this one wins hands down for location, size, and price. If everything checks out with the inspection, I'd have to say yes, too." They all looked at me.

"Majority rules," I said, but I softened it with a resigned little smile.

"That's a very Diva-esque sort-of yes," said Dad.

Mom whooped and tried to lift me in a big bear hug. My feet

stayed on the ground, so it was more of an enthusiastic upward tug, but I gave her an awkward hug in return.

"Okay, Mom—down, girl. 'Ro over there needs a hug, too."

"C'mere you!" Mom whirled around and throttled 'Ro. "I can't tell you what a great feeling I have about this place, guys! *So great!* What do you think of 'Pink Palace Party Planners' as my company name? With a pink flower logo where the petals are the four Ps in a circle?"

So much for getting the place painted, I thought.

"Subject to inspection, Rosie, right?" said Dad quickly. "Hold your horses until we get it inspected. For all we know, the foundation's rotting."

"It's not. It won't be."

"Well, we need to get it checked out, right?"

"You're right, Mike. Checked out," said Mom bravely, nodding.

"And we should probably keep our enthusiasm for the place quiet until we've made the final decision on it."

Riiight, I thought, looking at Mom.

"Mmm-hmm. Good plan. Keep it quiet." Mom nodded briskly.

The real estate agent came to the foot of the stairs. "So, any thoughts on the place?" she called up. Mom whirled around, her face radiant.

"Mom," I warned, "remember, we—"

"Oh, Erica," cried Mom, "we all *LOVE* it! We'll *TAKE* it!"

CHAPTER 3

Conquer, Achieve, Succeed?

O f course, uh . . . Diva—" the principal of St. George
Elementary, Mr. Harris, looked down at the forms on
his desk and gave a quick glance in my general direction "—will only have a few months of sixth grade before she
transfers to the junior high school next door."

"Plenty of time to make some friends," laughed Mom. "This
gal here will be having some BFFs over for a sleepover by the
end of the week!"

This gal stared down at her feet, felt her face flush, and
willed her mother to stop talking.

Mr. Harris gave a small, tight grimace, which I think was
his way of smiling.

"Ah, haha. Yes. True. And this young man . . ." He gestured vaguely at Hero.

"Hero," prompted Mom, shooting a proud glance at Hero.

Mr. Harris's eyebrows shot up.

"I just go by 'Ro," said 'Ro quickly.

Good plan, 'Ro, I thought.

Mr. Harris looked relieved. "Ah, *'Ro* will attend fourth grade for, well, let's see—April, May, and June." He glanced briefly at the top of our heads and cleared his throat. "Welcome to you both. It's only a few months until summer break, but I trust you'll be happy at St. George."

"Oh, I'm sure they will be," gushed Mom. She was sitting on the edge of her seat, and I had a horrified mental image of her dodging around the desk and giving Mr. Harris one of her smothering big hugs. "We moved because of my husband's business expansion, and what do you know? We buy a house right down the street from this wonderful school! Like it was meant to be!"

"Ah. Well . . ."

"And I know there are only three months of school left, but don't you think it's important that the kids start making friends, get used to their new school, feel at *home*, you know?" Mom pressed her hand to her heart.

"Of course, of course," Mr. Harris's eyes had wandered to the clock.

'Ro was completely silent and still, which was strange for him. Maybe he was feeling weird. I sure was.

I kept thinking how different this place was from our old school. Elmwood Elementary had been a chaotic, crowded, loud, messy place—children's artwork peeled off the walls in the dusty hallways, a dingy curtain hung lopsided on the stage in the gym, and kids swarmed all over the old playground equipment in the scrubby field. Mrs. Krantz, our massive, red-faced, redheaded principal, walked the halls in her sagging skirts and thick sandals, cracking lame jokes, breaking up scuffles, bear-hugging, nagging. Alexander and Maddie and I once made a list of "Krantzisms," words and phrases that Mrs. Krantz made up. Words like "boo-hinky" (any cut or bruise), "vroomish" (fast), or "blah-blahs" (a sad mood). My very favorite Krantzism was a phrase: "Stop that or I'll rip off your arm and slap you with the wet end!" She was so funny. Hilarious. She fit the school.

This school was not like that. At all. It was nothing like our old school. This school was as unlike my old school as Mr. Harris was unlike Mrs. Krantz. This school's cleanliness and orderliness was unfamiliar, its silence intimidating. The school office looked like a doctor's waiting room. It had vases of fresh flowers and a row of unscuffed leather chairs.

"Beautiful," breathed my mom when we first walked into the school. "Look at that! Will you *look* at that?" It was hard to see anything else but the tile mosaic that took up the whole wall. It was a mural of a guy (St. George, I guess) battling a fire-breathing dragon. On a banner waving off in the distance were the words CONQUER, ACHIEVE, SUCCEED.

No pressure.

Mom paused annoyingly every few feet to read out loud some quotations stenciled onto the school walls as we walked to the office.

"'Stories stretch the soul.' That's beautiful. And so true, *so* true. 'Books are the wings of the mind.' Lovely. Diva, you're a writer. Isn't that beautiful and true? Do you want me to mention to Mr. Harris what an amazing writer you are?"

"Absolutely *not*, Mom. Negative. Seriously: do not."

"Okay, okay," Mom laughed, throwing her hands up in the air. "You're right. Better they discover it for themselves." She winked at me and squeezed my arm.

I glanced now at quiet, serious Mr. Harris, trying to imagine him goofing around with the kids in the halls, kicking a ball at recess, joking about ripping somebody's arm off or hugging anybody in his whole life, ever. I couldn't do it.

He was listing the school's many extracurricular activities in his dry, bland voice.

". . . jazz band, running club, improv comedy club, culinary arts club, and of course our famous dramatic society for fifth and sixth graders. A fall production and one in the spring. Very well regarded, I believe. Very professional. Our director is

Professor Ducharme, from the University's Fine Arts depart-ment. This year is *The Wizard of Oz*."

Mom gave a little shriek. "One of my very favorites! I could sing every song!"

Mr. Harris looked alarmed.

"Mom," I muttered. Dear *lord*.

"*Mom*," 'Ro said at the same time. Nine years old, and even he knows that the principal's office isn't exactly the ideal place for belting out show tunes.

"Look at how these two boss me around!" Mom said happily, leaning in confidingly to Mr. Harris.

Mr. Harris squeezed out that smile that looked like it hurt. Then he escaped to find someone to show us around. As soon as he left the room, Mom swiveled to face us. She could barely contain her excitement.

"An actual *professor* directing the play! A *French* profes-sor! Oooh la la! Did you hear that, Diva? A professional, quality *production*, not one of those slapped-together little 'skits'"—she air-quoted dismissively—"they threw together at the last min-ute at your old school."

"Remember the one where the play had barely started and Warren Pitts threw up all over the stage?" laughed Hero. "Buck-ets of pu—"

"Okay, okay, we remember," I laughed. "Where Mrs. Krantz took over as the Lorax?"

That play had been legendary. Four parents had rushed the stage with paper towels, cleaning up and hustling Warren off. Everyone thought the play would be cancelled. The Truffula Trees and Swomee-Swans in their construction paper headgear stood there, frozen, until Mrs. Krantz puffed over, threw out her arms, and cried dramatically, "*I* am the Lorax and I speak for the trees!"

"I could barely stop laughing to say my lines, let alone feed Mrs. Krantz *her* lines," I said. "She actually did great. Really threw herself into it."

"You were *wonderful* as the narrator!" Mom said. "Improvising, pulling a triumph out of a disaster. The show must go on. You acted like a professional there. . . . Oh, Diva, I have a great idea." She grabbed me by the shoulders. "You have to audition for Dorothy! The lead role in your new school's play! You'd make friends with all the cast, who'll be so impressed that you—"

"Whoa, whoa, wait a minute, Mom! I haven't even gone to this school for one minute, for one second! We haven't even *seen* the place, and I'm supposed to walk into the lead role in the play?"

"Well, probably not the *lead*," said Hero, swinging his legs. "But maybe you could get a little part. Might be fun, Deev."

I glared at him.

"What?" he said, glaring back.

"Exactly," said her mother. "Hero agrees with me. Only why

not shoot for Dorothy? Why not? You know that story inside and out. Why not you?"

The question went unanswered as Mr. Harris ushered in the librarian, who had the tight-lipped look of somebody pulled away from real work to do something useless and annoying. She marched us through the school so quickly we were practically trotting to keep up with her.

"Cafeteria. Lockers. Gym through there. Theater."

I ignored Mom's silent, excited pointing at the theater behind the librarian's back. We sailed past the line of laminated posters of previous productions. *Aladdin, Beauty and the Beast, Annie* . . .

"Here's 6B. Mr. Khan's room. This'll be your daughter's class."

Before anyone could say anything, like, for example, "Whatever you do, lady, DO NOT—REPEAT, DO *NOT*—open that door!" the librarian had double-knocked and thrown the door wide open.

"Mr. Khan, sorry to interrupt. Just wanted to introduce your new student to the class. The one starting on Monday."

Silence.

The teacher turned from the SmartBoard. The eyes of the whole class shifted to the doorway. Mom gave me a little push in the back, which sent me stumbling forward a few awkward steps. I slid a hand over my ponytail, tucking in a few loose strands behind my ear. My ears felt burning hot, and I really hoped they weren't bright red. I didn't seem to know what to do with my arms and hands. I crossed them, then uncrossed them, then held one arm with the other hand, then thought that looked stupid, then let them hang straight, then finally just shoved them into my pockets. If I'd known I'd be paraded in front of the entire class, I wouldn't have worn my T-shirt with the apple core on the front, that's for sure. I'd had it for years, and while it was soft and worn-in and comfy, it definitely wasn't in any way cute or stylish. Mom said we were going to meet the principal. Just the principal. A short chat, she said. Ten minutes. A fun intro to the school.

Not having fun here, Mom. Not the tiniest bit of fun.

"Well, hello there," Mr. Khan said, his face friendly. "You must be Diva. Diva Pankowski?"

I will not be embarrassed by my silly name, I will not.

I nodded and smiled at him. I glanced over nervously at the silent class. They were all watching me. *Focus on the teacher-man,* I told myself. Mr. Khan reached out and shook my cold, clammy hand, then turned to the class.

"Can we all give Diva a big, St. George welcome?" The class clapped dutifully; I whispered "thanks," gave a confused little wave, and backed quickly into the hall, stepping on the librarian's foot.

"Sorry, sorry," I muttered.

The librarian marched us off to repeat the performance at Hero's class. Only 'Ro did things right. He said "Hiya folks!" and did a sweeping bow that had the whole class laughing and interested in meeting the fun new kid.

The end-of-school bell rang just as we were leaving the building.

"'Ro, want to go the secret way home? Along the river?" I asked, anxiously looking around at all the kids who might see us walk up the driveway to our new pink castle.

"Yeah, sure."

"Stick together, you two," said Mom, smiling. "I'll open the back door for you."

We ran down the street to the park, turned right, and followed a little footpath we'd discovered just after we moved in. It led to the back of the park into the trees, their new leaves a bright, spring green. Once we were hidden by the trees, I relaxed.

The feeling of peace and comfort and safety you get when you're in the trees. Another good one for my project.

The path led all the way along the sparkling river, separated by a bank of bushes and reeds. On our right were the fences of the huge houses of our new neighborhood. Our new neighbors. Our house was six long fences in from the path, but if you lost count you could always catch a glimpse of the pink glowing through the trees.

"Six!" said Hero, running his hand along the last neighbor's fence. "And here's our gate!" He pulled a wire that Dad had hooked up. "The house really does look like some kind of weird castle from the back."

"And this," I gestured to the river, "is the moat. The moat for the castle of Sir Hero the . . . what? Sir Hero the Kid? Sir Hero the Lame? Sir Hero the Goofball?"

"*Brave*," said Hero, squinting his eyes against the sun's reflection on the moat, "Sir Hero the BRAVE!" He dropped the monster-truck voice and continued, "Or the Smart. 'Smart' might work, too. I'll think about it." We locked the gate and walked through the yard, winding our way around the ridiculous little purple gazebo. It was circular, open to the air, with benches curved along the walls. A little table in the middle, and that was it. It had no purpose, other than being a place to sit in the yard. It was a secret, quiet place. You could always find an empty room in the house, but the gazebo was so peaceful and looked out over the trees and the river. Perfect for reading and writing.

"*There* you are!" Mom called. Her head bobbed over the top of the balcony outside the kitchen. "Kids, *kids*! Come quickly! We have company!"

Hero and I looked at each other. His brown eyes looked startled. Mine must have mirrored the alarm I felt.

My heart sank.

"Oh, no," I said. "Mom's been making friends."

CHAPTER 4

Enter Potential Mean Girl (Stage Left)

A girl and her mother were standing in our kitchen when 'Ro and I came into the house. Both of them wore yoga pants and hoodies, and each had long, curly reddish hair and slightly bulging pale blue eyes.

"Kids, meet our new neighbors!" Mom beamed at the two guests. "I nabbed them *just* as they were going into their house and said they just *had* to come and meet you both! This is Melinda—"

"Miranda," said the girl in a bored voice. She was picking at her nails and barely glanced at us.

"Mi*ran*da. Sorry," said Mom, laughing. "I'm so terrible with names. And this is her mother, uh—"

"Julie," the woman said. She looked at me and 'Ro, and added: "Mrs. Clay."

"Julie. Of course. I'll always remember that because of jewels or jewelry! Julie."

There was a little silence where more polite people might have realized they should ask *our* names. Mom rushed to fill the gap.

"And these are my wonderful children. That's Hero and that's Diva."

"Seriously? Those are their *names*?" That got Miranda's attention. She stared at us like we were museum exhibits.

"Miranda," her mother said in a flat voice. If that was supposed to be a warning that she was being impolite (which she was), Miranda sure didn't pick up on it.

"Those aren't *nick*names?" she continued. "They're for real their *names*?"

We're right here, Miranda. Honestly, how rude could this girl get?

"You want to see some ID?" I said. I smiled, though, like it was a joke.

"Interesting. Interesting names," Miranda's mother said, leaning back against the counter. She caught her daughter's eye, and they both smiled slightly.

"Thank you!" Mom said. "That's why we chose them! You only get one name, I always say, so it may as well be unique! Now their *middle* na—"

"Do you live right next door, or a few houses down?" I jumped in before Mom blabbed out our crazy middle names: Cleopatra and Augustus. Nobody outside the family needed to know those. *Ever.* I could imagine us going through the whole thing again, with rude Miranda saying, "*Cleopatra*? Is that seriously your middle name?"

"Next door," said Miranda, pointing a bored thumb over her shoulder in answer to my desperate question. She looked around. "We wondered if this pink house would ever sell. I mean, who would want to live in a pink house?"

"Mi*ran*da," said Mrs. Clay sharply. "She only means it's been empty for a while."

"Oh, I get that pink might not be for everyone, but I love it," Mom smoothed over the awkward moment. "Goes with my name: Rosie." She looked at Miranda kindly. "Would you like something to eat, honey?"

"I'm not hungry. Can I see your room?" Miranda turned and looked at me with those dead, bulgy eyes.

"I, uh, sure. It's a bit messy, but . . ."

Miranda was already running up the stairs. Hero looked at me and shrugged. His look said *good luck*.

"Sorry—Miranda's a little strong-willed," said Miranda's mom in a weary voice. She had a very unhappy face, I noticed.

"No, no, Julie, it's *fine*," Mom said. "It's fun for girls to show off their rooms! It's fun, right, Diva?" Mom looked at me, smiling and nodding.

Mom actually thinks that, I realized. She's such an open book. She actually, truly thinks (even hopes!) that Miranda and I are going to sit and swap secrets and giggle and do each other's hair and dance to music and become best friends and have sleepovers. Two minutes with Miranda and I already knew that none of that was ever going to happen.

That feeling of frustration mixed with guilt when your parent is clued out about a situation but really loves you so you feel mean getting mad at them.

"Sure," I said. "Fun."

I climbed the pink staircase and saw Miranda reflected in the mirrors dancing down the long hallway.

"It's one of those castle rooms, I bet," Miranda said, pulling open doors. "I always wanted to see inside those ones. Here?"

"No. It's there, up on the left."

I felt a mixture of resentment and admiration; I would never in a million years be as confident as this girl was, walking through a stranger's house, yanking open doors like she owned the place.

"Here. Here's my room," I said.

I loved my room. It was simple and plain, just my style. Mom and Dad let me choose any color I wanted and had the room painted before we moved in. I chose a deep blue called "Caribbean Surf." Soothing and calm like the ocean. I didn't even want to put up any posters, I loved the color so much. All of my books fit on the wooden shelves, with lots of room for more. And Mom had piled cushions on the window seat, creating a perfect reading and writing nook. It was a beautiful room.

"Oh, it's just a boring, little regular room," Miranda said, right on cue. She clearly had had no filter. "Blue. Looks like it should be your *brother's* room," Miranda said. "No offense."

"Blue's not only for boys," I said lightly. Every single word with this girl was awkward.

"I love green," Miranda said, talking right over me. "I look *great* in green."

Oookay, clearly no response required. I pulled my duvet straighter on my bed. Conversation with Miranda was like running uphill—hard and tiring.

"Do you go to St. George School?" I asked when the silence seemed to have lasted too long.

"Well, obviously. Everyone around here does," Miranda said, prowling around my room, picking up things and putting them back down. "It's okay. I mean, it's *school,* but it's okay. I like the plays. I always get the lead role. Annie, Jasmine, Anne of Green Gables. This year I'll be playing Dorothy. We're doing *The Wizard of Oz.*"

That's why her face looked familiar. That's where I

remembered her from. All those posters of the plays the school put on. Miranda had been in every one of them.

"Oh, I didn't know they'd picked the cast yet," I said. "The principal said—"

"They haven't. But I'll be Dorothy," laughed Miranda. "The director knows I have a bright future in theater. A *serious* future. Like, Broadway. I dance and I'm taking voice lessons. Want to hear something?"

Are you kidding? You're kidding, right? Or are you seriously offering to sing a song for me after knowing me for, like, three minutes?

"Well . . . sure, I guess—" I started to say.

"Hey, Deev, they're going." I turned with relief to see Hero standing in the doorway. "I'm supposed to tell you you're going," he said to Miranda.

"Oh, good. Musical theater claaaass," Miranda sang. She had a surprisingly lovely voice when she dropped her flat, bored speaking voice. *"So long, farewell, auf Wiedersehen, goodnight!* That's from *The Sound of Music.*" I knew that, but whatever.

Miranda patted Hero's head as she went past him.

"Bye, tiny little Hero!" she said as she danced out of the room.

"I can't *stand* her," said Hero, crossing his arms.

"Shhh. Not so loud, 'Ro," I whispered. "She's barely out the door."

"She's gone, *hopefully*. All that stupid singing. And I'm not *tiny* or *little*."

"I know, I know. She's just—I don't know—insecure." I didn't know if she was insecure or not (I actually thought not) but Mom always used that word to explain someone who was being a jerk.

"She's *rude*," said Hero. *Can't argue with you there, pal.*

"You think we can just stay here?" I asked him. "Or does Mom—"

"Diva! Diva!" Mom's voice floated up the stairs. "Come say goodbye to your new friend!"

My new friend. Is that what Miranda is? I bet you neither of us think that. I walked slowly down the stairs.

". . . and we'll have to get together sometime, Julie! Have a proper visit while the kids play." Mom was chatting away.

"Well, I'm pretty busy . . ." said Miranda's mother, her hand on the doorknob. "I've actually got a lot going on now. But maybe sometime. Anyways, welcome to the neighborhood and all that."

"Thank you!" said Mom. "And of course, Miranda's welcome here anytime. Anytime at all. Oh, here's Diva!"

"Bye, Miranda. Bye, Mrs. Clay," I said.

Miranda was already out the door, but Mrs. Clay waved quickly as Miranda tugged her out, too.

"Well," said Mom brightly. "Our new neighbors! Nice. Very

nice." She rubbed her hands together and gave me a smile. She saw my face and said: "Oh, Diva, they're *fine*. Maybe just a teensy bit insecure. Julie seems a little depressed, but maybe just a bad day. She said she'd mention the Pink Palace Party Planners to her friends, which was so kind of her, don't you think? I haven't even gotten the brochures back from the printer yet!"

I stayed silent.

"Not a bad thing to have a friend for when you start on Monday," Mom continued, slipping an arm around my shoulders. "Maybe Miranda will show you around and introduce you to all the kids at school."

Sometimes I wondered how Mom actually lived in this world. Was she insanely big-hearted or just monumentally clued out? Or possibly both? Anyway, she'd think I was being mean if I said: "Are you kidding, Mom? Miranda won't show me around. She would never, ever think of doing that. Introduce me to people? Don't make me laugh. If she even remembers me at all, she might mention 'that boring kid whose family bought that hideous pink house.' Can't you see that Miranda has serious mean-girl potential?"

So I stayed silent.

"Anyway," Mom said briskly, "I'm doing Tandoori chicken wraps tonight. Your favorite, kiddo."

But I couldn't concentrate on food. I was thinking about starting school on Monday. In three days. A school where

Miranda went. Miranda and people who were actually friends with Miranda. A school where Miranda was the star of every play.

The way I saw it, meeting Miranda had actually been a good thing.

Okay, maybe not a *good* thing. Maybe just not a terrible thing.

Because now I knew for sure who to avoid.

CHAPTER 5

Luxury Lunch Recess Hideaway
(I'm Being Sarcastic)

It was the third morning at my new school. My first impressions of Miranda had been confirmed. Not only did she not respond to my little wave when we were both walking to school, but she then sped up to make sure we didn't arrive at school together. She also totally ignored me when I said "hi" to her later in the hallway. Why did I even try? Who knows? I guess probably because she was the one person in a sea of strangers I'd met before. And it might have been nice not having to face them all on my own.

I slipped into class, slung my backpack over my desk chair, grabbed a book, and pretended to read as the rest of the class arrived for the day. I shook my hair out of its ponytail so I could hide behind its thick curtain.

That feeling of trying to be invisible in stressful situations.

School itself—the actual school part—wasn't so bad. Mr. Khan was really nice, and the subjects weren't difficult at all. I was even ahead in math. But the other part—the social part—was hard. Everyone but me had been there since the start of the year, so they already belonged to friend groups. It was awkward being the only one who didn't. I'm naturally kind of quiet, and so it's stressful trying to be outgoing and fun and social. Are there freakishly confident people in this world who actually enjoy marching right up to a group of strangers and introducing themselves? Okay, Hero. And Mom. But other than them?

Mercifully, Miranda wasn't in my class. Two of her friends were, though. Kallie and Miko. I only knew their names because Mr. Khan kept having to say "Kallie and Miko, focus please."

Kallie and Miko ignored everyone. They sat at the back of the class, flipped their perfect hair, and whispered to each other. My first day, there was an awkward few minutes when Mr. Khan had the whole class introduce themselves, student by student. Most kids looked over at me, even smiled, when they said their name. Kallie didn't look up from scribbling on her binder as she muttered her name, and Miko rolled her eyes at the ceiling while she said hers. Message received: new girl is totally unimportant.

After a couple of days of watching them, I became more convinced that they were definitely mean. But not *obviously* mean. Their meanness showed itself in a lot of little moments. For one thing, they didn't talk to anyone else. Ever. But they made comments to each other about everyone else. Kallie said "OMG, walk much?" to Miko when a boy tripped on his way to the sharpener. Or Miko loudly said "my eyes *hurt*" and actually put on sunglasses because another girl's neon-orange hoodie was apparently so bright. They'd mimic other kids or laugh at the way they talked. I could go on. Like I said, a lot of little mean moments, but they add up.

They were pros at using mind games. Which, when you really think of it, was a unique and very effective mean-girl strategy. Marks for originality, I guess. I saw the strategy in action yesterday, my second day of school, when I delayed going out for recess by pretending I couldn't find something in my backpack. Rummaging in your backpack is a very good time-wasting strategy. I highly recommend it. You appear busy, it's believable (who among us hasn't rummaged?), and it's boring, so nobody watches for very long or stops to calculate how long you've been rummaging. They just glance over, see a girl trying to find something in her backpack, then off they go. Nobody thinks: "Hey *wait* a minute—that girl has been rummaging in her backpack for *ten full minutes!*" They just move on.

Yesterday I'd rummaged so successfully that everyone in the class had gone out for recess by the time I'd looked up. Mr. Khan was away from his desk. I was all alone in the classroom.

I sat there with my backpack open on my lap (rummage-ready), in the peace and quiet, hoping I could sit there all recess. But then I heard girls' voices coming down the hall.

"Kallie! *Kallie!* Where *is* she?"

"Probably outside. Wait, is she still in class?"

"I'll check." Miko appeared in the open doorway. She was very pretty, with dark eyes and jet-black, long, straight, silky hair with no frizz at all. She had a rose-gold cellphone in one hand. She always had just the right clothes—stylish yet a bit edgy. Hair right, clothes right, everything, everything right.

But here's the mean part. Here's an example of the meanness. She looked into the classroom, looked right straight at me, called, "Nope, nothing. Nobody's here," and left.

Nothing. Nobody. Thanks, Miko.

Anyway, Kallie and Miko were a gang of two that grew at recess when they joined up with Miranda and two other girls I didn't know. Five people to avoid.

Recess and lunch were the worst times at school. That was when it was obvious that I didn't belong to any of the groups of kids who talked and laughed together, who played soccer or basketball, or who stood around the corner in the cool-kids spot even though it was technically off-limits.

This morning passed quickly, and the problem of recess was solved by Mr. Khan asking for volunteers to stay in to help organize a big shipment of books for the book fair. Two of us stayed in—me and a boy who'd sprained his ankle playing soccer. He was so nice. Funny, friendly, no pressure. No asking me about my stupid name or where I was from. Just goofy comments about the book covers. One had a cat on it, and he made me stack those because, as he said, "I'm a dog person, and my dogs would smell it on me." I wished I could remember his name from that lightning-fast intro my first day, but I still didn't know most of the kids' names in my class. He had longish, sandy brown hair and friendly hazel eyes behind circular glasses. There was a gap between his front teeth when he smiled, which sounds weird or even possibly unattractive, but it wasn't.

So morning recess was a definite win.

Now I had to worry about getting through lunch recess. Even though it was a beautiful spring day, I vowed I wouldn't go outside and wander the field alone again. Lunch recess had been dismal yesterday and the day before. I'd slunk along the fence on the outside of the school field, watching the others while pretending I wasn't. I finally sank down as far away from everyone as I could get and read my book. That book had saved my life.

I would have gone out into the field if 'Ro had needed me, if he'd been lonely, too. But 'Ro had already made friends, lots of friends. I'd seen him playing soccer in the fourth grade area yesterday. He saw me, too, and waved. I waved back and pretended like I was part of a group of girls ahead of me. I didn't want 'Ro to think I was pathetic. What could be worse than your nine-year-old brother's sympathy?

That annoying feeling of your younger sibling having everything way more together than you do.

Today, I evaluated my options while I slowly munched carrots dipped in hummus. I peeked up from my book and looked around the emptying cafeteria. Most of the kids had wolfed down their lunches and ran outside as soon as the bell rang for lunch recess.

Mr. Khan bustled through the cafeteria toward the library and glanced over at me.

"Still here, Diva? Why don't you get some sunshine? Catherine, Lila," he called to two girls near the door who were laughing and pulling on hoodies, "Diva might like to join you." He said this in a pointed, teacher-like way. It was as clear as if he'd shouted *"Hey!* Weird new girl's lonely. C'mon, help her out."

He was trying to help, but it made it worse to be a charity project. The girls looked over at me. Not unfriendly girls. Not mean girls. Just girls who wanted to get outside and talk to each other, or play soccer, or whatever. I'd already forgotten their names. Mom clearly wasn't the only one who was bad with names.

"Sure. You want to come outside with us, Diva?" They smiled as they said it. They were nice. Doing their duty. But I could tell they were probably just inviting me because Mr. Khan asked them to. I could feel my face getting hot.

I still had just a tiny bit of pride left.

"Thanks. Maybe I'll look for you outside. I just have to make a phone call first." I shoved the remains of my lunch into my backpack.

The student courtesy phone outside the school office was being used by a very young, visibly sick boy who seemed to be spending a long time convincing whoever was on the other end that he wasn't faking.

". . . I can hardly *breave* . . . [*cough, cough*]. No, I'm not! Not *this* time. My *froat's sore* . . ."

Trying not to think of the disgusting germs he was coughing into the phone, I skulked in the nearby library, strategically ducking and circling the stacks so as to remain invisible to people passing by. Yesterday, the librarian had let me stay for a while even though the library closes at lunch, but she eventually shooed me outside.

The sick boy had finally snuffled off to wait, red-eyed and runny-nosed, on the bench in the office. I sat down and wiped the phone down my jeans, then I bunched up a handful of my sweater and wiped it again with that. Finally, I pretended to punch in numbers, waited, and then talked animatedly to the dial tone and the wall.

"Oh, hi, Maddie." I always "called" Maddie, my friend from

my old school. Time-wasting strategy number two, when rummaging isn't an option. I missed Maddie and had called her for real a few times since we moved. She'd become friends with another group, which was good, which was great. I was happy for her. I was also selfishly worried that we wouldn't stay in touch, that she'd forget all about me.

"Uh huh, uh huh ... Sure, that sounds great!" I faked. "Who's coming? Oh, okay ... ."

I chatted happily with the dial tone for a few minutes until another boy came and stood nearby. He dumped his backpack on the ground, obviously waiting for his turn. I glanced over my shoulder, dismayed that I couldn't kill at least five more minutes with my super-fun, imaginary phone-friend.

"Mmm-hmm. Sounds fun. No way! Get out. Well, better go here ... bye!"

I saw by the clock near the front door that it was only 12:20. Fifteen minutes to kill. I didn't feel up to facing the field, trying to find those two nice girls from my class. Caitlyn? Lisa? I headed down the hall to the theater. I'd discovered yesterday that the stage door didn't shut properly. I'd opened it and peeked out onto the dark stage. Maybe today I could sit in the audience seats quietly in the dark and wait until the bell rang. That would be fine. Peaceful, even. I could definitely waste fifteen minutes there.

I went past the main theater doors, around the corner, and

climbed a flight of stairs with a door at the top. STAGE DOOR was stenciled on it in large, black letters. I pulled it open, startling a couple of teachers who turned, balloons in hand. A banner on the stage read BOOK FAIR. Forgot about that.

"Oops, sorry. Wrong door," I said, shutting it quickly. I stood outside the door, listening to the teachers resume talking and wondering whether I could sit here on the top stair. The voices got louder. They were coming toward the door.

I hustled down the stairs. Was there nowhere in this whole school that was private? Where I could sit by myself? I looked around, feeling desperate.

I saw the green door of the girls' bathroom across the hall. That would have to do.

The bathroom was empty. I chose the last stall, locked it, folded over a couple of lines of toilet paper, laid them carefully along the seat, and sat down. I stared at the gray door. Somebody had scratched a heart on the door with the initials A.S. + S.W. I wondered who they were, and whatever happened to A.S. and S.W. I thought of a bunch of names and finally settled on Alexandra Slade and Steven Wentworth. Alex and Steve. Were they in junior high, or maybe even in high school now, maybe dating? Or would they be absolutely horrified at the thought of dating each other? Sixth grade was a long way from high school. Somehow, I hoped it had worked out for Alex and Steve.

Looking to my right, somebody had written in Sharpie:

"You are your own dream come true!" That's the sort of thing Mom would love. I stared at it, thinking *no*, I most definitely am not a dream come true, mine or anybody else's. I kind of hated Sharpie-girl for making me think of how un-dreamlike I was.

I shut my eyes. At least it was quiet in the bathroom. Or it was for a while, until the door banged open and a group of girls came rushing in, laughing. I quickly tucked up my legs, my arms hugging my knees. I heard toilets flush and water run as the girls chattered.

". . . there. *Much* better. The smell of that hand sanitizer was making me *totally* sick . . ."

". . . and he said, like, 'I'm sure,' but he said it, like, in this super-mean way . . ."

". . . Oooh. New lip gloss? Gimme. C'mon! Oh, I *like*! What color is it? *Divine Diva* . . ."

"You're such a diva!"

"I am, aren't I?"

"Diva! That's that new girl's name."

I froze.

"The skinny one with the frizzy hair? Khan's class. Your class, Kallie! *Can* you imagine actually being *named* Diva?"

"Please. It's beyond stupid. It's like, 'I'm such a *Di*-va!'" Kallie sang out my name very dramatically.

"She's not a real diva," said a girl with a flat voice. "That would actually be interesting. She's just boring." I sat dead still in the stall at the end, knowing that last voice was Miranda's. "Her family bought that *hideous* pink house next door to us. Get this: her brother's name is actually *Hero*."

"No. Way."

"That's *way* worse than *Diva*. That's . . . wow. Messed up."

"Her mom's super-pushy," Miranda's bored voice continued. "Tried to get my mom to buy some birthday party supplies or something. My mom was like, 'Um, who are *you*?'" The other girls giggled.

I know for a fact that my mom would never have done that. She doesn't sell party supplies. She's a party *planner*. Either Miranda's mom was lying or Miranda was. I picked Miranda.

"On a less totally boring note," Miranda continued, "do we know when auditions are for the play?"

"End of the week, I think. You know you'll get Dorothy."

"Yeah. But who's going to get all the other parts? I mean, I want to know who I have to deal with. If, like, *Spencer* is the Tin Man or the Lion, I will kill myself."

"Might be. He can sing."

"And he's, like, three feet tall with those *lame* glasses . . ." She clearly did something with her hands, because the other girls laughed.

Spencer. Of course: *Spencer*. That was the nice guy who had unloaded the books with me during morning recess. He was almost my height, mean girls, not that that matters. And his glasses were cool.

"Anyway," said another voice. "The little dictator hasn't said when the auditions are."

"*Director,*" said Miranda.

"Dictator," emphasized the first girl. She went on in an elaborate French accent: "Zat is eet, Mees Smit! You 'ave no beezness near zis *play!*"

The door banged open.

Judging from the girls' dead silence, it was an adult.

"Oh, hi, Professor Ducharme," said Miranda. Her voice was completely different. Eager. Suck-uppy.

"'Ello, Miranda," said a cool, clear voice, with just a hint of an accent. "What is this? Some sort of club? Out you go. Shoo, shoo."

"Okay, but please just tell us when you'll be having auditions for the play. Please, please, *please?*" I could just imagine her opening her eyes wide and clutching her hands together.

"You can wait for the announcement like everyone else." The hard voice cut sharply across Miranda's wheedling pleas. "Now out, out!"

Footsteps, stifled giggles, and then the door banged. The sound of a tap running was blocked out by the loud buzzer signaling the end of lunch recess. As I bolted out of the bathroom, my eyes met Madame Ducharme's for a second in the mirror.

She looked startled, probably thinking she'd been alone in the bathroom. I slipped into the crowd of kids streaming in from the schoolyard.

I kept my eyes on the floor, watching the shoes of the boy in front of me. My heart gradually slowed down.

That relieved feeling of release from something really, really awful . . .

CHAPTER 6

I Realize I Am Not
Promposal Material

I won't be needing you for this one, pumpkin," Mom said. "It's not a kids' party."

Hero and I had been her party-planner helpers for years, her "Party-Partners." For parties involving adults, that mostly called for loading and unloading the van, blowing up balloons, stuffing loot bags, or folding serviettes.

"This party's a 'promposal.'" Mom smiled, expertly curling a bunch of long ribbons with one side of scissors and her thumb. Whatever that was, it was her latest booking, for Friday night. Judging by the huge calendar marked in red and the state of the basement, the Pink Palace Party Planners had lots of business in the few weeks it had been up and running. Labeled plastic totes lined the basement storage shelves. Some were marked normal things like *Streamers, Balloons, Party Favors,* and *Ribbons.* But many were in Mom-speak: *Do-Hickeys, Froo-Froos, Whatnots, Bling-Blings, Fancy-Schmancies,* and *Dingle-Dangles.* Everything was divided into sections, according to theme. We were in the "Romance" section of the basement (including engagements, weddings, anniversaries, and now, apparently, promposals).

"So ro*man*tic! The girl's mother has hired me to decorate the house before her special friend comes over and pops the question."

"Seriously? This is a thing? He's just *asking* her to go to prom? This isn't actually, like, their *prom*?"

"Oh, no," laughed Mom. "That would be a *way* bigger deal. No, this is just the asking part."

"Wow. That's actually a thing? I never even knew that was a thing. It seems weird to make a big deal, to actually have a *party,* because of a simple question. It seems like something you could do standing by your lockers or in the hall at school or something. I mean, quick. Ask, answer, you're done."

"I'm dying from the romance, Diva," Mom said, rolling her eyes and putting her hand over her heart.

I threw a fake flower at her. "You know what I mean. In *private,* just the two of them."

"The idea is for the party to be *public,* Diva, not private. I mean, it's a *promposal.*" Mom kept stressing that, annoyingly, like it was a real word.

"It's a party? They're having *guests*?"

Mom looked up from the fake flowers she was stringing into garlands.

"Of course! Food, music, cake, fireworks—the whole shebang. Oh, and they've hired a professional videographer." Mom said this as though that fact magically made this ridiculous thing legit.

"Videoing it? They're videoing a guy asking a girl to go to prom with him? That's ridiculous." Why did I feel about a hundred years old? Was there something I was missing here? This all seemed pretty grim to me. In fact, in front of guests, with the cameras rolling, it sounded like the least romantic thing in the whole world.

"Wait!" I said, startled by a sudden idea. "She's going to accept, right?" I said. "I mean, they're not decorating the house and filming it and everything and she'll be all, like, 'I'll think about it,' or 'Nah, I don't think so.' Right?" I don't know why that mattered to me. I guess I hated the thought of some guy getting humiliated in front of what sounded like a big crowd.

"I think that's the idea," Mom said, biting off a piece of thread. "Shame they both have acne." She made a pained face and gestured on her cheek with her hand. "Maybe the makeup artist will manage to hide it."

Makeup artist. I had no words for all of this. Promposal people clearly belonged to a different species than I did.

I helped Mom shake out the garlands of flowers, then circle them carefully around pieces of cardboard. I looked at the boxes stacked nearby. One filled with little bottles of bubbles. One with noisemakers. Streamers. Candies. "Promposal Pretzels," Mom pointed out. They looked just like regular pretzels to me.

"Seems a big deal for just a prom," I said. "I mean, I bet most people who go to prom together don't get married or anything."

"Probably not. But your dad and I did," said Mom, dimpling.

"True. But I bet you guys are pretty rare. And I'll bet you didn't have a stupid party when Dad asked you."

"Actually," said Mom confidingly. "I asked him."

"Hey, that's pretty cool, Mom," I said, looking at her with new respect.

"He was so *shy*," Mom sighed. "So I said to myself: 'Rosie, it's never going to happen unless you make it happen and ask *him*.' So I did." She winked at me.

I did not know this. *Mom* chased *Dad*. Weird.

"Did I ever see a picture of you at your prom?"

"Oh, gosh, no. And good thing. I had this *hideous* hand-me-down dress from my cousin. Dark green, of all un-prom-like colors. And clunky, old-lady sandals. Horrible, just horrible. Your dad borrowed a suit jacket from his uncle (too short in the arms; his wrists were sticking waaay out) and his shoes from his brother. They were about three sizes too big!"

Mom was smiling, looking off into the distance.

"Didn't matter, though, did it?" I said.

"What?"

"It didn't matter that you didn't have a promposal? That you didn't have a big party and a fancy dress?"

"Well, no, I guess not. We had such a fun time. Even with that ugly dress. Danced the whole night! Once we both kicked off those terrible shoes."

"So maybe all this *hoopla—*" I waved my hands at all the decorations "—isn't necessary if the two people really like each other. Right, Mom?"

Mom sighed and looked longingly at all her sparkly decorations.

"No, I guess it's not. You're probably right, Diva."

"So," I continued, leaning forward, "when I *don't* want a promposal party, when I totally refuse to have one, you'll understand, right? Right?"

"Oh, I'll under*stand*." She looked at me with her dancing brown eyes. "But then I'll throw you one anyway!" She laughed and hugged me.

Mission so not accomplished.

CHAPTER 7

Managing a Sentence of Normal Conversation

A t recess the next day, I was sitting under a tree pretending to read my book very intensely.

I'm fine, I told myself, just *fine*. I'm happy, *happy* sitting here all alone. Very restful.

I could have tried to find those two nice girls from my class who gave me the pity-invite yesterday, but how awkward would that be? I could just see myself wandering up to them, forcing a smile, them forcing a smile back as they remembered that Mr. Khan told them to play with me . . .

Why was it all so hard?

Hero raced by my tree with a group of boys running after him. How, in four days, did he have a whole herd of friends?

That feeling of envying your younger sibling, even though you're older and should have it more together.

Was it easier in fourth grade? He saw me and gave me a smile and a little wave, but he didn't stop. I don't blame him. Older sisters, like younger brothers, can be embarrassing at times.

I hoped he didn't pity me. I'd make a point of telling him later that I was just taking a break, having a little time to myself, finishing this really, really good book. Would he buy that, or would he just pretend to but secretly *not* buy it? Hero was pretty sharp.

As I was watching him and his little gang swarm the climbers, Spencer and another boy from our class came over and flopped on their backs under the tree. They'd been playing soccer, and both looked hot and tired.

"Shade!" Spencer said. "Must. Have. *Shade.*" He turned his head to look at me. "Sorry, Diva, only tree near the soccer field. Okay if we die here?"

"Haha, sure, haha," I said. Not my wittiest retort ever. Later, I thought I should have said something like "Only if I don't have to drag your bodies back to class." Or something like that.

That feeling of thinking of a smart or witty comment or a cutting retort way, waaay after the moment has passed . . .

They panted for a few minutes, and I pretended to read.

"What're you reading?" Spencer asked.

Not trusting myself not to do the ridiculous, nervous "haha" again, I just turned the book so he could see the cover.

"Hey! *The Wizard of Oz*! We're doing that for the play this year, did you know that?"

"Really? Wow. No, I didn't. What a weird coincidence." *Okay, calm it down there, Diva.* I didn't know why I was lying.

"Maybe you missed the notices. Auditions are on Monday," he said. "You ever been in a play before?"

"At my old school. Small parts. Mostly narrators." Could I *be* more boring?

"I always used to be the narrator," the other boy said. "I *hated* narrating. Yack, yack, yack. Sentence after sentence. And they take so long. Hours and hours. Mostly I just prayed for the thing to be over. In fact, I pretty much hate plays in general. It's all just made up, right?"

Spencer sat up.

"Wow, Jeremy, you couldn't be more negative. Unless you ended that last sentence with ' . . . and everybody dies.'"

"Haha," I yelped. Couldn't help it. He was *funny*.

"Acting is my thing," Spencer explained. "Basketball's his. So, Jeremy, let's just not go all negative. Because there's lots I could say about sweating in a gym for an hour trying to put a small ball in a *hoop* just a few more times than a bunch of other guys. Back and forth, back and forth. Like, what's with *that*?"

"Okay, okay. But at least there's some *point* to it. Like this next play, you're going to be—what? A lion? A guy made of metal? Why?"

"Tin. He's a Tin Man," Spencer corrected.

Jeremy looked at me as if to say "I rest my case."

"They're *symbolic* characters. It's a classic . . . *anyway.*" Spencer turned an exasperated face to me. "Diva, if you've acted before, you should audition! We need some new blood. The sheets are at the office. Just memorize the paragraph, come to the auditions with Madame Ducharme, and *boom!* give it all you got."

He made it sound so easy.

"I will if Jeremy will," I said. "I think he wants to be the tin-guy." Both boys laughed. There. Nailed a normal little bit of conversation.

Maybe I could do this.

CHAPTER 8

When You Are a Glitzy Giant Fish, Swim Away from the Mean Girls

I picked up the audition sheet. It directed "any student wishing to audition" (so far, so good . . .) to "memorize ONE of the following paragraphs and, **if they wish to try for a singing role**, to rehearse ONE of the songs from the play."

I brought the sheet home, laid it on my bed, and stared at it every so often as I wandered around my room biting my thumbnail. Did I really want to do this? Was it just opening myself up to humiliation? Or could it actually be a way to meet people and make some friends? Then I remembered Miranda. But she didn't *own* these plays. A lot of other people participated, too. People like, say, Spencer.

After ignoring, then circling, then fidgeting with the sheet for about nine hours, I sat down and actually read through the paragraphs. Dorothy's "no place like home" speech jumped out at me. I loved that one, and practically knew it by heart. Memorizing that would be simple. Easy. Practically done already.

And obviously I would have to sing "Somewhere Over the Rainbow," even though probably 98 percent of the kids auditioning would choose that one. With all the tempo changes, that song isn't quite as easy as it seems. It's taken years for Mom and me to perfect our version of it.

I paced around my room, humming the song. Then I started softly singing the words. Then gradually I found myself belting it out full voice, flinging my arms wide and twirling around as I sang the last verse. When I finished, I glanced down at the audition sheet.

I think I'd decided to audition for this play.

☆ ☆ ☆

Problem time: it was a very busy weekend.

"Deeeee-va!" Mom called. "Remember, the party tomorrow? I need you AND Hero. I had a great idea for this children's party. Big surprise!"

My heart sank. The children's parties were the worst. They all had themes—the "Arrr, Matey Pirate Party," the "Grrrrowling Grrrreat Animal Party," the "Clowning Around Circus Party," the "Pinkest Princess Party," and the "Rowdy Robots Party."

But the themes weren't the problem. The problem was Mom. She always had to take everything up a notch. It wasn't enough to have balloons and massive loot bags and endless totes full of games and prizes and piñatas. She needed *characters* to come and mingle with the kids. Costumed party-partners. Mascots.

Enter Hero and me.

True, we got paid for it, and I bought a lot of the books on my shelves with the money I made at Mom's parties. I didn't mind it so much when we started out. It was fun dressing up, fun being the big kid helping out with the little kids. But I was, like, eight then. Somehow when you're eleven, you're less enthusiastic about climbing into a gorilla suit (that costume is *so hot*). And by the way, they don't growl. I looked it up.

Mom adored each and every party she helped throw. Loved them. If we didn't go with her, she'd come home and gush over every detail, telling us how *wonderful* it all was. She honestly couldn't understand why I wasn't still as thrilled about every single party as she was.

"It's their *birthday!*" she'd say, as though some random stranger-kid turning six should of course have me leaping enthusiastically into a pirate costume, merrily mock sword-battling smaller pirate Hero. Other than the lame pirate, I've also been an unfunny clown (itchy, wild red wig), a not-so-pretty pink princess (crowns suck), a metal robot (can't sit down in that one), a giant hamster (fake fur: again, so *hot*), and a tall, bored tube of toothpaste. The toothpaste costume was a special request from a couple of dentists who wanted an oral hygiene–themed party for their daughter. Because we all know every kid is just *dying* for a party with a teeth-cleaning theme. But Mom made it fun somehow, and I dutifully stood around being toothpaste, handing out toothbrushes and helping with the tooth floss limbo game.

Mom made every single costume Hero and I wore. She's a wizard with a sewing machine, and honestly, if you could bottle that woman's energy, we could probably heat the house for a couple of years. Hero and I always had the elaborate Halloween costumes that other kids envied. No pre-made costumes off department store racks for us.

But right now, I was wary of Mom's great idea.

"*Just* advertised the 'Under the Sea Party' on the website last week, and *boom*! Got a booking for Saturday, right here in the neighborhood," she smiled. "So, Diva, you'll be a gorgeous MERMAID," she shrieked, shoving a slippery, shiny costume at me, "and 'Ro, you'll be a darling little RED CRAB!"

"Hey, do these pincers really work?" 'Ro scrambled into his costume, delighted with his enormous claws.

I quickly held my costume up, worried Mom might actually have gone full Little Mermaid with a clamshell bikini top. I would *never* have worn that. She must have known that because, thankfully, there was a loose, shimmery T-shirt for the top. The bottom was the real show-stopper. It was an enormous fish tail in gleaming greens, blues, and purples. I could tuck my feet in and be all swishy mermaid, but if I had to walk, there was a small hole so I could slip my feet out.

"Not much room for movement here, Mom," I said, taking teeny baby steps around the room while my fish tail dragged on the ground. *Whiff, whiff, whiff* . . . the costume made a swishing sound with every tiny step.

"Well it's not like you're going to be sprinting anywhere, kiddo," Mom laughed. "Oh, here's the pink wig to go with it. Aaaand the eyelashes. Aaand the glitter eyeshadow! You'll just lie on the couch looking gorgeous, swishing your tail, blowing bubble wands, and handing out gummi fish and candy necklaces. Okay? 'Ro will scuttle around helping me and doing the 'Crab Catch' game. Which does *not* involve actually catching kids. Just snapping at them. At the air *near* them. Got it, Hero?"

So, on Saturday, there I was, batting my shimmery eyelids and floppy false eyelashes, flipping my long, pink hair and swishing my giant fish tail. It wasn't terrible. The little birthday girl was totally, screamingly delighted with her personal mermaid, and kept running over and giving me hugs. How could I be a miserable mermaid with someone like that around?

There were about fifteen girls at the party, and judging from the laughing and shrieking during 'Ro's games, they enjoyed themselves very much.

The party was almost over when things took a turn for the worse. And by "the worse," I mean, *The Worst*.

I had just flopped awkwardly onto my right side to give my left hip a break when the doorbell rang. The nice mother running the party said, "Oh, that'll be Noriko's mom. She has to leave a bit early."

But it wasn't a mother who stood there in the doorway. It was a girl, about my age. Long, silky black hair. She turned her head, and I caught my breath in a horrified gasp.

It was Miko. And then, like the universe didn't think that was *quite* horrible enough, Miranda joined her at the door. Both girls came into the house.

"Noriko," Miko called to one of the little girls who must have been her sister. "C'mon. Gotta go."

My mind started racing, trying to figure out a dignified escape. Dignified. Who was I kidding? I was a giant fish. Better not shoot for dignity. Any escape at all would do.

There was a group of kids between me and Miranda and Miko. And lots of balloons. So I was shielded a little. But it would be a total disaster if they saw me. Recognized me. I remembered how they'd gossiped about Mom and me that day when I hid in the school bathroom.

I could only imagine what they would say about pink-haired mermaid-girl to the rest of their little pack. How they would all laugh. I could imagine them telling other sixth graders, who would tell *other* sixth graders, who would . . .

Bathroom, I thought. That's where I should go hide, right immediately *now*.

I slid off the couch in an awkward, thrashing roll, like a fish caught in a net. I pawed desperately with my feet to find the hole in the costume so I wouldn't have to slither, fish-out-of-water style, out of the room. I finally found it and shoved both feet through.

It seemed to take me about a year to struggle upright, but when I did, I moved as fast as I could. I was heading down the hall to the bathroom, *whiff-whiff-whiffing* with each tiny baby step, when I heard my name.

"Diva!" a voice called. *Oh, no. Mom.*

Go, Diva! Get your fish tail in gear! Go! I went faster. *Whiff-whiffwhiffwhiff.* This hallway was endless. I stumbled and toppled over, then struggled back to my feet, my wig sitting crooked on my head.

"Deeeee-va!"

Faster, faster! Whiffwhiffwhiffwhiffwhiffwhiff. I pumped my arms. In my head, I was practically sprinting, but in my feet, I was moving ridiculously slowly.

Come on, Diva—move! Move!

I looked over my shoulder just as Mom appeared at the end of the hallway.

"Ah, *there* you are, you gorgeous mermaid, you! Look who's here! It's Miranda! And another friend, uh . . ."

"Miko," said Miko in a totally dead-bored voice.

I turned, snatched off my pink wig, and leaned against the wall nonchalantly. So that way, nobody would notice my gigantic fish tail, right? Riiiight.

I gave a casual wave.

"Oh, hi." I tried to match Miko's bored voice.

"Wow, that's *some* costume," said Miranda. She looked at Miko and they both turned to look back at me, small smiles on their faces.

"Very . . . aquatic," drawled Miko.

Mom clearly thought this was polite interest, two nice girls, friends of her daughter, genuinely appreciating a really artistic costume.

Mom didn't have a clue.

Mean people don't need to say much. They don't actually need to say anything. Sometimes we non-mean people forget this. We sometimes think all meanness is out there in the open. We think it's all sneering comments, mocking insults, shouts, and punches. It's not. Meanness can be there in a long look. It can be there in a smirk. A small, shared smile. All the unspoken undercurrents of meanness were lashing out at me now, as obvious as if Miranda and Miko had shouted them and laughed out loud.

They were enjoying this, enjoying me burning with embarrassment, enjoying the feeling of catching me doing something stupid and humiliating.

Silent bullies are still bullies.

"It's been fun," said Mom. "Diva's been giving out gummi fish and shell necklaces! And blowing lots and lots of bubbles. Underwater theme you know." *Stop, Mom. Just stop talking.* "And the birthday girl had her own personal mermaid! Doesn't she look amazing?" said Mom, not picking up on one, single, screaming clue.

Miranda looked me up and down.

"A-*ma*-zing," she said. Mom surely heard that dripping sarcasm.

I looked at her. Nope, apparently not. She was smiling as though we were all having just the best time. A bunch of BFFs hanging out.

"Diva's got loads of costumes," Mom said excitedly, digging me deeper into the pit.

"*Loads* of them. How fun," said Miranda. She looked straight at me, that little smile appearing again.

"But this one's new!" Mom kept right on going. "But where's the wig? Oh, there in your hand. The pink wig really sets it off, girls. Show them the wig, Diva."

"Yeah, show us," said Miranda. Her bulgy blue eyes were dancing.

That's it, I thought. I'm not going to model this ridiculous wig for two girls who I'm pretty sure are semi-openly ridiculing me now, and 100 percent certain to ridicule me later as well. This whole thing was already bad enough.

I'd had it with all three of them.

"You want to see the wig?" I croaked loudly. "Sure. Here you go!" I threw it down the hall toward them. Then I turned, quickly whiffed into the bathroom, and slammed and locked the door. I struggled out of the stupid, stupid mermaid tail like a toddler in a tantrum kicking off her snow pants. It was a relief to be free of it, to be able to move normally in my leggings.

As I straightened up, I caught a glimpse of myself in the bathroom mirror.

Great, just perfect.

I looked *way* worse than I could have imagined.

I had pulled my black hair into a tight bun this morning so it would fit under the wig. It had been perfectly smooth, even sleek. But when I snatched off the wig, wild, frizzy strands of hair had escaped, standing up all over my head. There was a red, itchy-looking line straight across my sweaty forehead from the pink wig. My pink lipstick was smudged down on one side of my mouth like a sad clown. One of my long fake eyelashes had become snarled up like a spider, and tears tracked smeary glitter down my cheeks.

I looked like some sort of nightmare-zombie-mermaid. A mermaid who would send young children screaming, splashing frantically to the shore.

I smothered a panicky laugh with my fist.

Then I closed my eyes and took a deep breath.

And I sat down on the toilet and waited.

That feeling where you desperately want to be in your bed, with the covers pulled tight over your head . . .

CHAPTER 9

The Wise Man with the Animal Stickers Gives Advice

I t was a short, silent van-ride home. 'Ro didn't know exactly what was going on, but he knew *something* had happened. And he knew it wasn't good. Probably because Mom shushed him when he started talking, silently pointing to me and mouthing "crabby."

"I *saw* that, Mom! I am *not* crabby," I yelled.

Honestly, could anything be more enraging than being called crabby when your life was collapsing?

"Speaking as the only legit crab in the van, I agree," said 'Ro, snapping a pincer in the air. "*You're* not the one who's crabby." He almost made me laugh. Almost.

I practically leaped out of the rolling van when we pulled into the garage. I ran all the way up the stairs, scrubbed my glittery face clean in the bathroom, and then crawled into my bed. I pulled the covers up over my head and stayed there a long, long time. Trying not to think, trying not to re-live the squirming embarrassment, trying not to utterly dread going to school on Monday. Trying to clear my mind. Trying to be calm.

I kept telling myself that I wasn't important to those girls. They weren't important to me. But I was going to be stuck with those people for all of junior high. Maybe even all of high school.

I lay curled up under my blankets in a lump of pure misery.

Finally, my stomach rumbling, I wandered downstairs. No sign of anyone around in the huge house, and that was just fine by me. I stood at the counter and ate a cold piece of leftover pizza. As I munched, I noticed a light on in Dad's study across the hall from the kitchen. I went over and tapped at the door.

"C'mon in," he called and looked up from a small desk covered in papers. "Oh, hi kiddo. Mom and 'Ro went to soccer registration." He rubbed the back of his neck. "I, uh, heard the party was fun."

I didn't answer. *If by "fun" you mean giving two girls a truckload of ammunition to make my life even more miserable than it is now, then sure, Dad, it was a blast.*

"Part of it was okay. Part of it . . . oh never mind. I just want to forget it."

I looked around Dad's office. There was a sleek new corner

desk running almost the length of the room. Matching bookshelves and cabinets lined the walls. Two leather chairs sat in a corner with a coffee table in front of them.

"Wow," I said, perching on a stack of boxes, "I haven't been in here since all this furniture was delivered."

Dad looked around uncertainly.

"Yeah, lots and lots of stuff. Mom picked it all out. It's really great quality. Solid wood. They built the shelves right in there, see? Professional job. Mom's right; it's about time I had a proper office, somewhere I can be organized, spend more time at home, even have a client pop by once in a while. Not just the hole-in-the-wall I've always had."

I looked down at the small, beat-up metal office desk he was sitting at.

"So why are you still at your old desk if you've got all this fancy new stuff?"

He sighed. "It takes me a while to get used to new things. To tell you the truth, I work pretty well at this desk. Did you know this was the first desk I ever had? When I started up the company. Back way before you were born."

"Jeez, old." I smiled. "I like your stickers." I pointed to the side of the desk. It was covered in animal stickers.

"Well, you and 'Ro decorated it back in the day." He laughed, shaking his head. "Maybe they're part of the reason I like this old desk." He wheeled his chair out. "History. And look here—remember this?" He pointed to a huge smiley face scratched on the inside of the desk. "Remember?"

I laughed. "I remember. I was, like, four and used a key when you weren't around. Scratched that in so that you'd have—"

"—happiness all the live-long day!" Dad finished, slapping the top of the desk. "Your exact words." He smiled at me, then smothered another yawn.

"You're tired," I said. "Working hard?"

"Always, always," he sighed. "Shouldn't complain. Business is booming. How are things with you?"

"Not so great, actually. Shouldn't complain, either. But I'd really, really *like* to complain."

Dad laughed. "Well: shoot."

I picked at the box I was sitting on.

"Oh, I don't know, Dad. School's just . . . hard. Well, not *school*, but the other kids. The people." He nodded and waited. I loved that about Dad. He let you stammer and struggle and he didn't make you feel slow or awkward because you did it. He just listened. Mom would have been bouncing around the room, making suggestions, finishing my sentences, planning, trying to force things to get better. Dad just sat quietly and let me talk.

"Like, for example, there's 'Ro. Running around with a group of friends already, and I can't figure out how he does it. I'm not—I don't have—I haven't really met many people yet. Almost none, actually. I'm not really great with people, you know. Or even *good* with them. On a scale of, say, excellent to brutal, I'm definitely at the brutal end."

Dad looked skeptical.

"No, Dad, it's true. I'm not like Mom or Hero. I'm more like you! No offense, but we both kind of suck socially."

"I prefer to think I have a quiet dignity rather than 'suck socially,' as you so eloquently put it," Dad said, air-quoting the phrase with his fingers.

I laughed.

"Well, see how far having 'quiet dignity,'" I air-quoted back, "gets you in sixth grade, Dad. I'll answer that: not far. Because people want you to be funny and loud and cool and smart and pretty and all sorts of things that I probably don't even *know* about."

I picked at the box. I was tearing quite a strip off of the old cardboard.

"How did *you* get through school, being quiet and shy?" I asked him.

Dad blinked. "Well, I don't really know. I guess I played sports."

"Okay, not an option for me. You've seen me throw. And run."

"You throw and run just fine. Stop running yourself down. What I'm saying is that I got *involved* in something, and the friendships flowed from that. Is there anything you could get involved in at St. George?"

"Well, I could audition for the play, I guess."

"I was hoping you'd say that. You've always enjoyed being part of the school plays. And you're *good.*"

"Thanks. Weird how sometimes it's easier getting up in front of a gym full of people than talking to one single person. You know?"

"I don't, actually," Dad admitted. "The thought of getting up onstage terrifies me. In fact, it's a recurring nightmare of mine. Pushed out onstage, no idea what the play is or what line I'm supposed to say." He shivered. "Now your mom . . ."

"She would have *loved* being in plays, Dad. She's a natural performer." I smiled, thinking of Mom singing all those show tunes.

"Maybe you are, too."

"Maybe. There's just such a good feeling when you've all pulled together rehearsing, and then it's opening night and the room gets quiet, and the lights go on and the play starts. It's exciting."

"Sounds like you should do it."

"Auditions are Monday. I brought home the sheet to practice. It's *The Wizard of Oz.*"

"Hey, you must've seen that movie a million times. You probably know it by heart. You've got all day tomorrow, so *practice,* and give it a shot!"

"But maybe I won't get a part," I said. "This is a *way* different school than Elmwood was, Dad. *Way* different. There's this semiprofessional director who sounds totally intimidating, they actually print *posters* of the plays, they rehearse for months. There are tons of kids, and I bet there'll be lots of good actors." I didn't mention Miranda, but I was thinking of her.

"Maybe you won't get a part," said Dad, somehow not understanding that what I needed him to say was "Of course you'll get a part!" Like Mom would have said. And then I wouldn't have believed her.

"But you'll have *tried*," Dad continued. "You'll have gone after something you wanted. Isn't that worth something?"

"I don't know, Dad. It's complicated. Some of the people that might be in the play aren't the nicest. At all. Some are, though." Yes, I was thinking of Spencer. "I just don't know."

"I do. Try out for the play." He said this, pointing a finger at me, mock-stern. The laying-down-the-law role was so not Dad that it was funny.

"Okay, boss-guy. I will," I said, pointing right back, mock-serious. "But only if you keep the desk."

We smiled at each other.

"Deal."

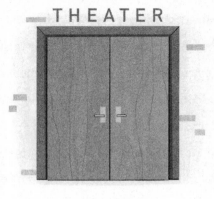

THEATER

CHAPTER 10

Not Quite the Grueling Ordeal
I Had Feared

Auditions were Monday after school, so I had the whole day to really wind up into a nervous wreck. My hands were ice-cold as I packed my backpack. I rehearsed Dorothy's speech in my head, as I'd done all day.

I paused at the last line. It was Dorothy, back from her adventure, remembering that while some of her experiences hadn't been all that great, most of them had been beautiful. I'd like to think that just about sums up life. I seemed to be waiting for the mostly beautiful part. But there had been a hopeful episode today. One of the nice girls in my class, a small girl with dark curly hair, saw me looking at the audition sheet at recess and asked me what paragraph I'd chosen. She'd picked Dorothy's speech, the same as I did. A few of her friends joined in, saying which parts *they* were going to read, and they talked and laughed about what could go wrong and how scared and nervous they were. I was pretty quiet, because I couldn't think of anything funny to say, but for most of recess I was part of a group!

I went down the hall to the theater, running through the speech over and over again in my head. Home. It was all about home. About coming home, about Dorothy finally finding her way home.

I tried to think about how I would have felt, being away from Hero and Mom and Dad. I tried to think about what "home" was to me. Home was a deeper idea than just a place you lived. For me, home wasn't the pink house yet, and it wasn't the small house we'd left anymore. It was my family, and the feeling of belonging to them. With them. *That's good: hold on to that feeling during this audition*, I thought. The feeling of home.

The hall leading to the theater was lined with kids waiting to audition. It was loud with nervous chatter and laughter. I saw Miranda and Miko sitting on the floor with their eyes closed, looking like they were trying to block out the rest of us. I slid down with my back against the wall and sat on the floor as far away from them as I could get. I'd successfully avoided those girls all day. There was one episode that made me think I wasn't going to get off so lightly, though. At lunch, Miko and Kallie walked past my desk, and Miko said, just loud enough so that I knew she wanted me to hear, "Something smells fishy around here."

Such a small thing, but it was a reminder. We know. We remember. Don't forget that we know.

I prayed the auditions would be alphabetical and those girls would be done and gone before I had to go in. But waiting until the Ps would be torture, too. At the rate I was biting my fingernails, I would have none left at all and would have started in on the skin around them by the time I was called. I hoped they wouldn't start bleeding. Sometimes you just rip a little piece of skin off, and it bleeds ridiculously for a while. I pictured stumbling into the audition all blood-spattered, and the mental image was enough to make me stop biting.

I was pretending to read my book when that nice girl from my class slid down beside me. We smiled nervously at each other.

"Lots of kids," she said, pushing up her glasses and pushing back her curly hair. "Shoot. I'd hoped there wouldn't be so many. I'm Shaya, by the way. You got introduced to, like, a million of us, so you probably don't remember."

"Shaya," I repeated, so I'd remember it. "I'm Diva. Or Deev."

"I actually like Diva," she said. "Unique."

"Same with Shaya, actually."

"I always have to spell it out, though."

"Same here!"

We laughed at this tiny little link.

"Have you been part of the plays before?" I asked.

"Nope. This is my first time auditioning *ever*. And I think I'm only doing it because my brother Jeremy *doesn't* do the plays, and it would be nice to do something he doesn't do better than me. And I'm so nervous I think I'm going to throw up."

"Me too," I said. "At least we can throw up together."

She laughed. "Double-puke. Never been done!"

Shaya's last name was Abrams, alphabetically one of the first to be called when that big theater door opened.

"Good luck," I whispered as her name was called. "Break a leg, I mean."

"You too!"

Spencer came down the hall as she was going in, and he gave her a high five.

He caught my eye and smiled. I smiled back.

Talking a bit with Shaya, a smile from Spencer. Maybe this wasn't going to be such a scary ordeal.

☆ ☆ ☆

By the time my name was called, the crowd in the hall had thinned out.

I scrambled to my feet and went in. The door closed with a *thunk* behind me. I walked across the stage to where a woman was standing. The acoustics in the theater were very good; each step I took across the stage sounded clearly. You could almost hear the hushed silence when I stopped.

"Hi. I'm Diva Pankowski." Was that raspy voice mine? I tried to clear my throat a little, which is hard without making a sound at the best of times, let alone when your every breath is being amplified outrageously.

My breath was coming quickly, like I'd sprinted across the stage, and I didn't know what to do with my arms. It was awkward just leaving them hanging, but it seemed rude to cross them or shove my hands into my pockets. What was left? It was totally *not* me to stand there with my hands on my hips. That was more of a Miranda pose, I thought. Confident. Sassy.

Madame Ducharme was the woman from the bathroom, but I hadn't gotten a good look at her then, because I was running out the door. As she looked down at her clipboard, I studied her. She was an older woman with spiky black hair and red lipstick lining very thin lips. She wore a long, black dress, high-heeled shoes, and lots of jangly bracelets on both wrists.

"Well, *Diva*, you certainly have a theatrical name," said Madame Ducharme. She smiled at me. A nice smile, not like she was making fun of my name.

"Haha, well, my parents wanted something unique—"

"So let's see whether you live up to it." Madame Ducharme swept over to a chair and collapsed gracefully into it. I wasn't sure when to start until she raised her eyebrows and threw out her arm. "Proceed. When you're ready."

"Okay," *Calm, slow, with feeling,* I reminded myself. It was good advice that I somehow totally ignored. Was that my high, shaking voice rattling off Dorothy's speech at breakneck speed? Too fast. Way too fast. I gulped as I finished it, and looked at Madame Ducharme miserably.

"That was way too fast, right?" I said. "Sorry."

"You're nervous. It's okay. Calm. Breathe. Once again. Feel it."

Breathing actually helped. I don't think I'd breathed once all the way through that speech.

Focus, I thought. *Think about Dorothy. Think about Home.*

I recited the passage again, trying to infuse it with life, with meaning, like I did when I'd rehearsed in my room. My calm, beautiful, blue room.

I stopped, and there was a silence. Madame Ducharme looked at me with her head tilted to one side, a quizzical look on her face.

The silence lengthened.

Does she think that was horrible? Oh, why am I even doing this? For Mom and Dad? To try to fit in somewhere, anywhere? Because I was a big shot at the stupid little plays I'd been in before? To see if I could compete with the other kids in this school? With Miranda?

"Hmmm. Much better." Madame Ducharme stood up and came over to me. She pulled back her shoulders, and lifted her chin, encouraging me to do the same. "Posture. There. Now, 'ow about a song? Or no?"

"Sure," I said. Deep breath. I sang a few lines of the song, expecting her to stop me. She raised her eyebrows but let me sing the whole song. I closed my eyes and imagined I was singing with Mom in the kitchen, like we'd done so many times making dinner.

When I finished, Madame Ducharme had a strange expression on her face.

"That was . . . unexpected," she said. "Very, very nice. Your singing voice is different from your speaking voice. Rich, bold, deep, deep, deep. Unusual. You are a bit of a mystery, Diva."

Then she surprised me.

"You're new to this school. Good for you to audition for the play. That took *guts*." She nodded briskly and stood up. "Thank you. *Next!*"

CHAPTER 11

Birthdays: The Most Dangerous Day of the Year

W e'd only been in Castle Pink-a-Lot three weeks when the birthday talk started. *My* birthday. April 16. Two weeks away.

Always, every year, a very dangerous day.

Mom was extra-super-squealy excited about birthdays. It was irritating sometimes, but I understood why she was like that. My mom was an only child whose parents died in a car accident when she was four. If that wasn't sad enough, her grandparents, who raised her, were really old and very, very strict. Like, "lights out at seven p.m.!" strict, chores before school strict, plastic covers on the furniture strict, no birthday parties or sleepovers strict. She desperately wanted a kitten, and they finally gave her a small, homemade cat stuffie (it's kind of creepy, but she still has it). Maybe her grandparents loved her but didn't want her to become spoiled. Maybe they thought they were doing the right thing. But poor Mom—I always picture a little girl (okay, I picture Hero, but with longer, curly Mom-hair) who longed for fun and music and people and excitement. For birthday parties and a kitten to cuddle.

Anyway, thanks great-grandparents-who-I-never-knew, because Mom had a total, urgent need to do better for me and Hero. Not just a little better. Waaay better. Professional-party-planner better.

Hero and I didn't have regular birthday parties like other kids had. Ones with a few friends and maybe some burgers and cake and a movie. I loved those kinds of parties. Low-key, easygoing, fun. Maybe you'd run around at some park, but mostly you just joked around and laughed with a few friends. The best party I ever went to was Helen Mendoza's in fourth grade. She had three girls over, and her mom and dad made some delicious Filipino food—dishes they grew up with. Then—and this was the super-fun part—Helen pulled out a trunk with a ton of fancy dresses that her mom used to wear when she was a singer on a cruise ship! And we tried them all on and piled up our hair in outrageous and unflattering styles and clomped around in too-big sparkly shoes and sang along to Taylor Swift songs and had *so* much fun. That was it. Simple. Just a trunk full of old clothes. Best party ever.

Hero and I never had simple birthday parties. We had extravagant birthday parties. Over-the-top birthday parties. Looong birthday parties. Bowling and pizza and cake, then laser tag and swimming and build-your-own sundaes and a bouncy castle and a two-night sleepover with face painting and crafts and movies and scavenger hunts and blah, blah, blah.

I would never have told Mom this, because it would have hurt her feelings terribly, but those parties that she worked so hard at always started out great, but into day two, everyone just wanted it to be over. I know I did. Even kids you really like can get annoying at two a.m. when they're still talking and everyone's had too much sugar. I'd calculate how long it would be before I could be alone in my room, reading a book in bed. Mom would never have understood that.

Hero loved the parties, of course. Mr. Personality enjoyed every minute of them. He once told me he wished his birthday party could last all birthday week. "Birthday week" was a phrase in our house, because our own personal celebrations lasted at least that long. Pancake breakfasts and surprise gifts and scavenger hunts and favorite dinners and on and on.

But no chance of all the hoopla this year. I was so relieved.

"So, Diva, what are we doing for your birthday?" Mom asked as I did my homework at the kitchen table. "I have a few ideas . . ."

I looked up, alarmed.

"No, Mom. Hold it right there. No ideas. Do not even think of *one* idea . . ."

"Just a few. Little ones!" She playfully squinted and measured an inch with her thumb and finger. "Tiny!"

"Mom. I don't really *know* anybody yet," I said, thinking of the nice girls in class. I'd only spoken to a few of them. A few words here and there. "There's nobody I know well enough to invite to a party, so—"

"You have Miranda! Right next door! I keep telling you that you can always ask her to pop over."

"Mom, you don't understand." I ran my hands through my hair in frustration. "I don't . . . she's . . . we don't really get along. She's got other friends, okay? We're *not* friends, so stop thinking that we are! She never even talks to me."

How could I tell her that it was crystal clear that Miranda wasn't remotely interested in being friends? That she seemed to go out of her way to avoid me, literally turning her back on me when we caught each other's eye at lunch recess. And when Miranda didn't completely ignore me, every time she passed me in the halls or by the lockers, she gave me a look that said: "I belong here. You don't. And we both know it." Or, worse than just a look, she'd make rude comments under her breath to one of her friends about pink houses or mermaids or party-planning. Just loud enough so I could hear.

Mom pulled up a chair and sat down.

"I'm sorry, honey. I didn't realize that. I guess I hoped—well, anyway. It's been difficult, huh?"

"Sort of."

"It's hard meeting new people sometimes," she said. I nodded. "But it's only been a few weeks! It will come, Diva. You're such a wonderful person, so much fun, so smart! So much to offer. It will happen." She grabbed my hand and squeezed it, hard. She had a look on her face that hurt—desperately wanting to do something to help me but knowing that she was powerless.

"Thanks, Mom," I said, pulling my hand away, but patting hers so I didn't hurt her feelings. "It's okay. Really. I'm fine. It's just, coming into a new class near the end of the year, people have formed their groups already. Some kids have been nice and friendly, but there are no birthday-party level friends, if you know what I mean. It would be totally awkward to invite them *here*, to our house. I mean, you need to be at a certain stage of friendship for that. I just don't know them that well. Do you understand?"

"Of *course* I do, pumpkin," murmured Mom.

"So none of your over-the-top birthday hoopla is going to work this year."

She started to protest, but I talked over her.

"And I'm *fine* with that, Mom. Really. A party with just our family. That would be nice for a change. Just us. Something small and simple. I'm turning twelve, right? Getting too old for birthday parties anyway."

"What? *No!* Don't say that. You're *never* too old for birthday parties!" Mom smiled brightly, but I could tell she was worried and feeling sorry for me. "Things will improve, Diva, I just know it. I have a *great feeling* about that. A great feeling."

She meant well, but I wished she hadn't said that.

CHAPTER 12

A Roadmap to Humiliation

". . . and our final announcement: the results of the auditions are in, ahhh . . . and the cast of our play, *The Wizard of Oz*, has been selected. At recess or at lunch *only*, and in an orderly fashion, ahhh . . . students may check the list posted outside the theater to see if they, ahhh . . . made the cut, as it were."

Our principal, Mr. Harris, was the only person I knew who could suck the life out of such an exciting morning announcement. I remembered Mrs. Krantz, the principal from my old school, shrieking into the mic: "Woo-hoo! Roles for the play are out! No sniveling if you didn't get the part you wanted. Suck it up, buttercups! We can use *anybody and everybody* for sets and costumes."

My heart started to pound. The list was out. It was actually posted outside the theater at this very minute. Just a single piece of paper that could change my life at this school. Was my name on it? Did I want my name to be on it? I honestly didn't know. I guess I did, because if I *didn't*, why was I so stupidly nervous right now?

That feeling of desperately hoping for something, but telling yourself repeatedly you don't care at all, not even one little bit.

Shaya turned and caught my eye. She crossed her fingers and smiled in a nice way, as if to say "I hope we both get parts." I liked her. I made a mental note to try to find her at lunch recess.

I tried to concentrate on math and waited until the middle of next period, Health, to ask if I could go to the bathroom. The bonus was that I got a break from a cringey video on "personal hygiene" narrated by some enthusiastic nurse. She was going on about acne care when I left.

The hallways were completely empty—exactly what I wanted. The very last thing on earth I could bear was to stand with a crowd of other kids, all of us jostling to see whether we made the list, everyone else knowing who made it, the ones who did shrieking and high-fiving, the ones who didn't trying to act like they didn't really care. All of that would happen at recess. Right now, the coast was clear.

I had to hurry. The theater was way farther away than the bathrooms, on the other side of the school from my classroom. I ran-walked down the long, empty hall, my footsteps slapping loudly. Finally I turned the corner to the theater doors. There was a long piece of paper taped to the right door.

My heart did this weird squishy thump, which under other circumstances might have worried me. I took a deep breath.

I'll take a quick peek, see that I'm not on the list, then I can just relax and get on with my life.

I looked at the sheet, headed *"The Wizard of Oz* Production: Cast List." On the left, a column of names, linked by a line of dots to their role listed in a column on the right. Pretty simple, even for somebody whose insides were shaking like jelly.

I ran my finger down the names on the left. It started with Miranda Clay. She was Dorothy. Of course she was. Spencer got the part of the Wizard, which made me happy. Then some other names I didn't know. Miranda's friends were on there, too. Kallie got the Scarecrow, Miko was the Tin Man. Sliding down the list, I saw Shaya was a Munchkin.

My finger stopped at the last name. The very bottom of the list. Diva Pankowski! I made the list! I got a role in the play! My breathing quickened. I slid my finger over to the right, following the trail of dots.

Only when I got there, the words didn't make any sense.

I went back to my name, put my finger on it, and followed the dots over to my part.

How . . . ? What . . . ?

Underneath Dorothy, the Wizard, Glinda, and the rest of

them, underneath even the Munchkins and the Jitterbugs and the anonymous roles like the three beauticians and two Oz men, there was my role. My big debut at St. George. My part in the play.

And if it wasn't a mistake, if this wasn't some horrible typo or terrible misunderstanding, it was going to be so humiliating.

I wanted to snatch the paper right off the door and crumple it up, so nobody else would see.

But I turned and walked quickly back to class.

☆ ☆ ☆

That night at dinner, I could tell that my parents wanted to ask straight out whether I got a part in the play. But I think they realized I wasn't very happy, either. I knew they were looking at me, and I saw them glance several times at each other.

Hero was completely oblivious. He chatted on about his soccer goals, the cool new robotics club he went to, his friends. When he stopped talking long enough to take a bite, Mom jumped in.

"So. Diva. You've been pretty quiet. Anything new today?" she asked.

"Nope." Eyes on my plate, I pushed a piece of fish around and around.

"Okay, that's gotta be a lie," Dad teased gently. "Nothing new? At all?" He gave me a quick, worried look. The worry made my decision.

I put down my fork.

"Okay," I said loudly, "you should probably know. The list of who got a part in the play was posted. And I got a part—"

"Woo-hoo!" shrieked Mom, dropping her knife and fork in a clatter and pumping her fists in the air.

"No, Mom, would you *listen*? This is definitely not a woo-hoo moment. It's so stupid I don't even know what to think about it."

"What, the *play* is stupid or your *part* is stupid? And if it's a part, how can a *part* be *stupid*?" Hero asked, his mouth full.

"'Ro: chew. Diva, no part is small in *The Wizard of Oz*, if that's what you're worrying about," said Mom. "Every part is im*por*tant. Every. Single. One."

Mom and Dad stared at me, clearly baffled.

"What part, exactly, did you get?" Dad asked.

Here goes . . .

"The Yellow Brick Road," I muttered. Saying it out loud was even more embarrassing than seeing it written down.

Hero snorted out a laugh. "*What?* The Yellow Brick Road? The *road*? How are you supposed to be the *road*? You must not talk at all, because a road can't talk. What can a road do, even? What kind of a part—"

"Hero, please, you are *not* helping." Dad said.

"No, actually, Dad, let him laugh. *Everyone* will laugh. He's right. Who ever heard of someone playing the part of the Yellow Brick Road? It's so stupid. It's a thing! It's something that's *painted on the floor*! It's tarmac! It's definitely not a part."

"Well, Professor Ducharme must be interpreting the play so that the Yellow Brick Road is somehow brought to life," said Mom calmly, picking up her knife and fork and starting to eat. Surprised, I looked at her.

"What do you mean?"

"Well—" she swallowed a mouthful "—when you think about it, the Yellow Brick Road is a powerful symbol in the story. It's something Dorothy is told to follow because it leads to all the good things. It leads Dorothy and the gang to Emerald City."

"Mom's right," said Dad. "We've seen that movie a hundred times. It's true—it's the path to the prize."

"So maybe Professor Ducharme thought that the Yellow Brick Road would be a *character* the others follow," said Mom, pointing at me with her fork. "Maybe you get to sing the 'Follow the Yellow Brick Road' song! One of my favorites."

Mom was actually making me feel a little bit better about this. Or if not better, at least a little less miserable.

"Maybe . . ."

"Professor Ducharme knows what she's doing," said Mom. "She's a professional. A professional *professor*. Trust her."

"Mom's right," said Dad, relief in his voice. "Absolutely."

"I don't know," I sighed. "Maybe you're right, Mom."

"Well that'll be a first," laughed Mom. "Oh, and congratulations, Princess! First part at your new school. Go in there with your gorgeous head held high."

"Yep, take the high road," said Dad. "No pun intended."

"The high *road*. Get it, Diva?" said 'Ro, ready to explain the lame joke further.

"Yeah, I got it, 'Ro. Everybody got it."

I almost laughed.

Almost.

CHAPTER 13

People Are Talking
(*About* Me, Not *to* Me)

I don't actually know if Miranda and Miko blabbed about me being a part-time pinkish mermaid, or if people heard about me *also* being a yellowish Yellow Brick Road (take your pick for which one sounds stupider), but I had the feeling all the rest of the week that people were talking about me.

That sounds paranoid, I know. It sounds like I'm being a bit of a drama queen, actually. But the truth is, I'm almost sure of it. I'm about 94 percent sure I'm not imagining it. Maybe even 96 percent.

I'd moved on from being The Invisible Girl, the ghost who haunts the bathroom and the tree in the school field. But I was still used to an attention level of around . . . well, zero. Maybe a few degrees above zero attention. Even now, when Catherine and Lila in my class included me at recess, I mostly watched and listened. I hung out with them but didn't actually feel part of the group yet.

I didn't get a chance to try to make friends with Shaya. I had it all planned. I'd just walk up to her totally casually and congratulate her on getting a part for the play (meanwhile praying that she hadn't seen what *my* part was and ready to laugh about it good-naturedly if she had). But she went home sick on Tuesday and wasn't at school for the rest of the week.

But then weird things started happening. A group of kids I walked by totally stopped talking. I'm not making this up. There was that electric silence that there should be a word for (mental note for my book) where everybody knows that the person being talked about just walked by, including the person who just walked by. I knew immediately they were talking about me. I knew even before I passed by them and heard one of them whisper *"That's her."* That's who? *Me?* Why me? That's the crazy Yellow Brick Mermaid?

If that were the only incident, I might have shrugged it off. New girl stuff. Nothing deeper than that. But other things happened as well.

For example, another time, I just happened to look up in class and two girls who were looking at me quickly looked away. But I wasn't doing anything at all, so why should they be looking at me? One shoved a paper under her binder like she didn't want me to see it. So maybe they were not only looking at me, but also passing notes about me. It was unsettling.

And *another* time at recess, I noticed two boys in a different sixth grade class talking. Total strangers, but I saw one glance over at me and do a head-tilt in my direction to his friend. As if to say "That's her. There she is." The other boy turned his head and looked right at me, then turned back and said something to make the first guy laugh. I pretended not to see, but I did.

I know, I know: these are all small things, just quick glimpses, impressions—barely-there stuff that you think might be all in my imagination. But added up, they seemed big. I couldn't shake the feeling that something was going on, that people knew something I didn't. Something that wasn't good. And I felt like I was groping around in the dark, trying to figure it all out.

The only bright spot in a weird, weird week was when Spencer stopped at my desk on Friday before heading out for recess. I was rummaging in my backpack at the time.

"Hey, Diva, did you get a part in the play? I didn't get a chance to see the whole cast—everyone was there at recess on Monday, pushing and shoving . . ."

"Haha. Yeah. Crowded!" *Breathe.* Full sentences now. "A part? Yes, I got a part. Just a little one."

"Hey, congrats! Which—"

"How about you?" I cut in before he asked which part. I was

determined to keep the words "Yellow Brick Road" a secret for as long as I could. "I'm sure you got a part, right? What did you get?" Like I didn't already know. But I didn't want *him* to know that I knew which part he got.

"I got Oz!" He looked genuinely pleased that I'd asked, which made me think that he hadn't only asked me so that he could tell me which part *he* got. Which is something many people do. Which also made me think that I needed to stop overthinking everything and calm down.

"Wow, congratulations! Excellent. Like, really, really . . . wow. Lots of, you know . . . talking . . ." I made a weird motion with my hand like that would clear it up.

Arrgghh. Lines. They're called *lines*. My brain obviously knew this but blanked out at the crucial moment.

"Oh, well," he laughed. Either he was amazingly easygoing and didn't notice how awkward this conversation was, or he was phenomenally kind and was just taking pity on the weird girl. "Just gotta practice. One line at a time, right? Well, I gotta go. Oh, I'll see you at the—" his eyes opened wide and he stopped "—at rehearsals," he said hastily, pushing up his glasses. "I'll see you at rehearsals."

And he turned and practically ran away. Maybe, I thought unhappily, he just realized how hopelessly awkward I was, or he just didn't want to talk to me anymore, or he didn't want other people to *see* us talking together, or he saw what was supposed to be a quick, two-sentence chat turning into a longer, more awkward conversation.

None of those were good options. I wanted to sink through the floor.

Anyway, it was a complete and total relief when school was finally over for the week. Our pink castle had never looked so good. Mom hadn't booked me for any parties this weekend, probably because she knew I was still "crabby" about last weekend's mermaid fiasco. I didn't even have any homework.

Our first rehearsal for the play was on Monday, so I did have that to worry about, but maybe I could reserve all day Sunday for worrying and nail biting, and just chill Friday night and Saturday. I thought of how soothing it would be to write in the gazebo, with just the trees for company. They sometimes whisper, but trees never stare.

"Where's Mom?" I asked when I came downstairs after dumping my backpack in my room and changing into my oldest, most comfortable sweats. Dad was looking in the cupboards and Hero was doing homework at the pink counter, sitting at a stool and swinging his legs.

"Doing a party," said Dad. "Engagement or something. I can't remember."

"Maybe it's that horrible promposal party," I said. "Did you guys hear about that one?" I told them about it and was glad to hear they thought it was as awful as I had.

"I would *hate* that," said Hero. "And I like parties."

"Yikes. That would have made me run a mile back in the day," Dad said. "Anyway, I'm making spaghetti." He stirred some sauce in a pot. "Then I thought the three of us might go play badminton tonight. You guys versus your old dad. Like old times."

"I'm in," said Hero quickly, shooting a look at me. "Sounds like fun, huh Deev?"

"I don't really feel like going out," I said. "Besides, where would we even play badminton around here?" We used to play badminton at the open gym nights at our old school. Epic, loud, thrashing battles that left all of us sweaty and breathless.

"Looked into it, and there's a big rec center pretty close. Ten-minute drive. Please? I haven't had much time with you guys lately."

"C'mon, Deev," Hero pleaded, "we're *so close* to kicking Dad's butt! And it's Friday—he's probably tired and worn out from the week. It'll be an easy win. Pleeeease?"

"Okay, okay," I laughed. "But I'm pretty tired, too." I thought about how this rec center was close. Only ten minutes away. Close might not be a good thing. Close might mean that kids from school hang out there on a Friday night. Another reminder I was spending my weekend with my little brother and parents. Sigh. "Really tired. Maybe just a *quick* game."

Dad looked so relieved that I was glad I agreed to go. He must have been worrying about me more than I realized.

Both of us were worriers, built to brace for the worst. It was exhausting. Mom and Hero were different. They just sailed through life with a smile on their faces, expecting wonderful things to happen. And they usually did.

I looked over at Hero. He was spinning on the counter stool, his head lolling back. Then he stopped suddenly and peered in the oven.

"Yum, garlic bread," he said happily.

Totally worry-free.

CHAPTER 14

A Totally Unexpected Total Disaster

"Wow, this is absolutely *nothing* like our old school's gym," I said as we pulled up to the huge rec center. "Other than maybe that they're both technically buildings."

"Nice. I like it. Pretty glitzy and new, huh?" said Hero.

"Maybe it won't have *quite* as many dust bunnies to slip on as Elmwood's gym," Dad said.

"Lots of people here. Lots and lots," I murmured. The parking lot was packed, and a steady stream of people were coming and going from the building. I was beginning to wish I had stayed at home.

"It'll be *fine*," said Hero. "A place this size, they've probably got, like, four gyms." He gave me a quick look. "It's gonna be *so* fun!"

Dad pulled out his phone and punched out a text. "Sorry—work. Okay, aaand *done*. Pitter, patter, let's get at 'er.'"

Walking into the busy, brightly lit building, I wished I'd worn my newer, less comfortable sweats. The crowd seemed to be mostly families and older people, but still—people. People with eyes, people who judged you. I caught glimpses of a few kids my age and was pretty sure a couple of them went to my school. I smoothed my hand over my hair.

"So let's get—" I choked back the rest of the sentence, which was "this over with," and substituted "cracking," which was a lame Dad-word like "scoot" or "shebang," but whatever.

Looking around idly, I suddenly froze. I saw a boy run in the front doors and down the hall to the right of the front desk. I didn't see his face, but I could have sworn it was Spencer. Same hair, same running hunch I'd studied during the recess soccer games while pretending to read my book under the recess tree. I only caught a glimpse, though, like a one-and-a-half second glance. I was probably wrong. *Please let me be wrong*, I thought.

I felt a little guilty about squirming in embarrassment at the thought of anybody at my school seeing us. But let's be honest: it wasn't exactly the coolest of Friday-night activities to be teamed up with your little brother to play your *Dad* in badminton. Especially the way we played. There was usually a lot of yelling and thrashing and flailing around in our games (mostly by me, but still). I looked down and noticed Dad was wearing his ancient, "lucky" bright blue and neon-orange badminton shoes. Great, just great.

Why couldn't there ever be a situation, really *any* situation, where I looked cool? Like, for example, maybe riding a horse. People always looked impressive on a horse. Or laughing in the middle of a group of friends at the mall. Or talking on a rose-gold cellphone in a perfect outfit while flipping my perfect hair. Or being interviewed on the news for rescuing somebody from a disaster (flood? tornado?). Any non-humiliating, non-embarrassing, very cool situation. I wasn't picky.

"Down thataway to the gym," said Dad, pointing with his racquet down the same hallway potential-Spencer just ran down.

Please don't let Spencer and a group of guys be in the gym. I remembered that Spencer's friend Jeremy played basketball. The memory of that conversation came flooding back like the voice of doom. What if they all hung out on Friday nights shooting hoops?

Oh please, no.

"Wait. Dad, don't we have to pay?" I asked, stalling. "I mean we can't just walk in without paying. So let's just get in line like everybody else, right?"

"Already got a membership," said Dad, dashing my hopes of a long wait in the entrance lineup, which might even have been so long that we'd pack it in and go home. "Let's go." He and Hero walked quickly through the main foyer over to the hallway. I hung back.

"Jeez, sometime this *century*, Deev," complained 'Ro. "Come *on*."

There was no sign of Spencer down the hall, so I relaxed a bit.

"I think it's in here," said Dad, pulling open a door on his left.

"I don't think so, Dad—it's totally dark. Why would a gym be dark?" My eye fell on the little rectangular plaque beside the door. It said PARTY ROOM 2.

I had a momentary thrill of pure terror.

Party Room?

Oh dear god, no . . .

But there was no time to do anything or say anything, let alone turn and sprint back down the hall. It all happened so fast. The door opened to the blackness, then Dad reached out and snapped on the lights.

"SURPRISE!!" The room erupted with the sound of what seemed like hundreds of people yelling and blowing noisemakers. A few nearby people threw glittery confetti. Lights flashed from a phone camera.

"Whaa—" I stumbled backward into Dad. Hero grabbed my hand and dragged me into the room. A blaring "Happy Birthday" started up from the sound system.

"Haha! It's your *birthday party*, Deev!" screamed Hero above all the noise. "A week early! Haha—*gotcha*! Total surprise! You never suspected a *thing*." He and Dad high-fived.

No, 'Ro, I really, really didn't suspect a thing, up until that last split-second. I didn't suspect this even a little, tiny bit. Not after I told Mom specifically and repeatedly and in great detail how I absolutely, positively did not want even a small party, let alone a Times-Square-on-New-Year's-Eve-level party. No, probably stupidly, this party actually *did* come as a total surprise.

I looked around at all the kids in the room. Most of them had gone back to talking or running around.

I didn't trust my voice to speak. I looked over at Dad. He smiled anxiously down at me.

"Surprised? Happy?"

Happy? *Happy?* My first thought was not, strangely, one of total betrayal: that he knew about this party and lied to me to get me to come. That was bad enough. No, my first thought was way lamer. It was: *He knew about this massive party and let me wear my OLDEST SWEATS. How could he?*

"I—I—"

Mom ran over and practically tackled me in a giant bear-hug.

"Mom, what—why—"

"At a loss for words? That's always a good sign of a proper surprise!" Mom looked absolutely elated. Music started blaring from the sound system, and a DJ in sunglasses announced:

"This one's for Deeeee-va," and gave me two thumbs-up. Bewildered, I gave him a weak smile and a thumbs-up back. I was grateful for the music. It would have been horrific to have total silence, everyone staring and hearing Mom gushing.

Mom gestured to the crowd. She raised her voice above the music.

"We invited the whole sixth grade from your school! Five classes! Happy birthday, Princess! You said you didn't want to have a house party, and I totally understood that. So I thought this would be a better idea. More public, less private! Isn't it *fun*?"

I looked down at her with a frozen smile on my face.

"*Fun*," I repeated. It was more of an incredulous question, but Mom took it as an exclamation.

"Good! That's the birthday girl spirit!" she said. She gave my arm an excited, painful little squeeze. "Let's go mingle!"

That awful, guilty feeling of helplessly almost hating your parent and knowing they don't have a clue at all.

CHAPTER 15

DIVAPALOOZA!

C'mon," shouted Mom above the music. She grabbed my hand. "Let me show you the stations!"

Stations? What on earth . . .

She dragged me into the crowded room. It was enormous, decorated with hundreds of bobbing gold balloons and criss-crossed with silver streamers. There was a banner spanning most of the high ceiling, with the word *DIVAPALOOZA!* spelled out in huge black letters, outlined in tons of gold and silver sequins, glittering in the strobe lights as the banner waved.

"Kept the color scheme to gold and silver!" Mom yelled into my ear. "Classy! Grown-up!"

I stared at the banner. *DIVAPALOOZA!* If I ever live this down, it will be a total and utter miracle. It will take some sort of national-level disaster to make other kids forget about this one.

My stomach felt tight and my hands were ice-cold. This was a miscalculation of sixth grade on an epic scale, with me as the guinea pig. Mom and Dad (mostly Mom, I'm betting) threw this party because they know how socially inept I am. I wasn't making friends, so they thought they'd introduce me to all these kids in my new school, and let's be honest, hoped the party would impress them. They were trying to show them how much fun I am, how party-worthy I am.

No, Mom. No, Dad. What everyone will think is very different from that. Were you ever in sixth grade? Best-case scenario is that everyone will think I'm this completely spoiled brat who demanded an over-the-top Beyoncé-level birthday party. The middle-case scenario is that they'll think the new kid has a loud, tacky, and pushy family. But the rock-bottom, very worst-case scenario is that they'll think the new girl is such a loser that her family needs to buy her friends.

There was no good angle on *DIVAPALOOZA!*

I feverishly made a mental note to Google "homeschooling" when I got back to our house.

Mom dragged me through the noisy crowd. I reached back and ripped the elastic from my ponytail, and let my hair shield my burning face. There were a few sort-of familiar faces—kids from my class, kids I'd seen at the auditions for the play or in the field or in the halls, but most of them were total strangers.

I hung back, but who knew Mom's little hand could have such a wicked-strong death-grip? Couldn't squirm out of that one. It was as if she sensed I wanted to run to the nearest bathroom and lock the door. She led me around tables with vases of fake flowers and foot-long candy skewers, silently pointing them out, grinning, and giving me the thumbs-up sign.

I finally understood what she meant by "stations" when we got to the far side of the room.

"I couldn't decide which to do, so we did them all!" shouted Mom.

First up was the *Krazy Karaoke* booth, where a boy I'd never even seen before belted out songs the DJ was playing into a very loud microphone while busting out some totally lame dance moves. He and his friends were having a great time, apparently, judging from the scream-laughing.

"Woo-hoo," shouted Mom. "He's *good.*" The microphone did that high-pitched scream mics sometimes do, and we covered our ears and ran on.

The *Dandy, Dandy Cotton Candy Shoppe* was next, where a man with a big cotton candy machine whirled out huge swirls of pink and blue.

"One for the birthday girl, Ted!" yelled Mom. The man smiled and passed a pink cotton candy to us over the heads of a lineup of kids. I saw their faces. Everybody resents somebody who butts in line, even if she is the birthday girl, the Diva of this Palooza.

At the *'Stache Station*, there were dozens of fake mustaches, beards, and eyeglasses. Huge wooden panels had been painted with headless characters (a business suit, a clown, a doctor, a baby, an astronaut, etc.) where kids could take a picture with their head on top. Get it? You're a big baby, but you have a mustache! How weirdly, randomly fun! I guess it wasn't totally lame because a group of kids was there, trying on mustaches and taking selfies. But I think they were doing it sarcastically, in a way that made fun of it. One of the kids was in my class. I think her name is Alexandra, but she was looking the other way.

The DJ was screaming something into the mic about a "prize scramble." He pulled out a bucket and started throwing handfuls of little objects into the shrieking crowd. One of them hit me on the side of the head. It was a small deck of cards. It dropped to the ground, two girls lunged for it in a scuffling match, and one of them ran off, holding it high in the air.

"Isn't that fun?" Mom yelled, laughing as she watched a group of kids tussling for the loot on the floor.

"Not really," I muttered. "Hey, whoa, that one was close. That guy almost got kicked in the head!"

Mom wasn't listening to me.

"Don't worry, kids," she shouted. "More party scrambles

to come! And if you don't get anything, there are loot bags to take home!"

I wondered, with a sick feeling, how much Mom and Dad had spent on this party.

There was a whole gallery of games: tossing beanbags into a giant gorilla's mouth (*The Great Gorilla Gobbler*), a timed basketball shot game that you played against an opponent (*Shootout Showdown*), a golf ball putting station (*Par-T-Putt*), a grab-a-stuffie machine (*Stuffie Snatcheroo*), and a balloon-animal making station (*McSqueakz Balloonz*).

"I *really* wanted to have a dunk tank," shouted Mom above the music, which had started up again, "but can you believe they said no? Water! Might ruin the laminate. And there was good old Dad—all set to be the dunkee!"

Two girls from my class ran by with little stuffies. They accidentally bumped into me and shouted, "Sorry." They saw my face and yelled, "Hey, happy birthday, Diva!"

"Thanks," I yelled back. "Total surprise! I had nooo idea!"

I don't think they heard me, but I thought I better get that out there right off the bat. I knew nothing about this wedding-sized party. That was true. The girls pointed to their ears like they couldn't hear me, but even so, somehow I felt a little better. They looked like they were having a good time. They even gave me little waves as they ran off.

Mom pulled me over to the photo booth. There were trunks

full of costumes, tables lined with hats and costume jewelry and long feather boas.

"Isn't this super-fun?" she yelled.

The booth was packed. Even a group of moms were glamming it up with the boas and taking selfies.

Mom stopped, shouting excitedly with the other moms. Before I turned away she'd grabbed a boa and was right in there posing for pictures with the rest of them.

Seeing my chance, I slipped quickly away into the crowd. I kept my head down as I passed by the balloon volleyball court but glanced around to see if maybe I could find anybody I knew.

Uh-oh. There were some people I knew. Miranda and Miko's group was standing against the far wall. Kallie was pulling candy off a skewer and dropping the ones she didn't like on the floor. Miranda and two other girls were doing what I guessed were ballet-style leaps and twirls, and Miko was texting.

I turned with the urgent instinct of an animal running from predators and smacked right into a group of boys.

"Sorry," I muttered, but none of them even turned around.

I finally fought my way to a less-crowded area of the room and sank down into a seat in the shadows, partially hidden by a giant speaker.

I saw Hero racing around with two other kids his age. They'd managed to snatch some of the gold balloons and silver streamers.

I saw Dad laughing with a group of kids as he "reffed" the balloon volleyball game. Spencer was on one of the teams, laughing with a group of girls.

I watched everybody who came to my birthday party while the deafening music pounded endlessly. Songs I never listened to or had never even heard before.

Everyone seemed to be happy and laughing and enjoying this loud, loud party.

Everybody but me.

That feeling of being lonely, lonely, lonely in a crowded room at your very own ginormous birthday party.

CHAPTER 16

The Party Lasts Several More Years

ll of a sudden, the music stopped.

"Sixth grade party animals!" yelled the DJ. "It's time to get our birthday girl up here to blow out some birthday candles!" He started up a chant.

"Di-*Va*, Di-*Va*, Di-*Va* . . ."

I swallowed and mentally calculated the sprinting distance to the door. Too far; right across the room. Why had I not escaped to the bathroom sooner?

Mom was at the mic now.

"Deeeeee-va, where are you? Everybody, I need your help. Help find Diva!" She said this like it was some fun, Find-the-Diva game.

I needed her to stop talking before she started telling the stories about when I was a little girl and used to hide in various

120

places (the pantry, under tables, behind curtains), reading books. Bear in mind that I was two at the time, but the stories always ended with me being discovered and saying irritably: "Tan't see me!" Adorable, maybe, when told around family. Around the entire sixth grade? Not so cute.

I needed this to be over as quickly as possible. *I will go and blow out candles*, I thought. I will endure everyone dutifully singing "Happy Birthday." But if anybody so much as *thinks* of giving me the bumps, I swear I will fight like a wildcat.

"I'm over here, Mom," I called, coming out from behind the speaker. "I was just . . . back there." I started weaving my way through the crowd to the DJ platform. I wished there was still the cover of music—because all of a sudden, even with the murmur of talking, the room was way too quiet.

"Ah, I think I see her," said Mom, shielding her eyes and squinting theatrically. "Yes, it's definitely her. The Birthday Girl! Get ready to sing 'Happy Birthday'!"

Miranda gave me a long look as I walked by her, then turned and whispered something to Miko. I looked down at the ground the rest of the way, achingly conscious of my old clothes, a trickle of sweat running down the side of my face. The room felt very hot, what with all the people and the lights and the crippling embarrassment.

"Here she is, here she is! Diva has ARRIVED!" Mom was trying really hard to make this a special moment. Hero high-fived me as I got to the platform, and Dad patted my shoulder, looked anxiously at my face, and whispered, "Everything okay, Deev?"

I nodded and climbed up the three steps. Mom swept me up in a smother-hug, clanging the microphone against my shoulder.

"Whoops, sorry folks!" she laughed. "Well, Diva, twelve years old! Is there anything you want to say to everybody? Anything at all?" She smiled and held out the microphone.

I couldn't believe she would do that. Put me on the spot. What on earth should I say? Other than maybe: *Why are you doing this to me, Mom?*

I had a horrifying mental image of myself smacking the microphone out of her hand and running, screaming and crying, for the far door. But I didn't. I thought about what a disaster this party was, but it flashed through my mind that I'd come through disasters before. Like when Hero broke his arm and I ran all the way home for help. Like the performance of *The Lorax* at my old school, where Warren Pitts threw up all over the stage in the first act.

That's it, I thought. Treat this as a play. My part is the happy birthday girl, delighted at this lovely surprise party my parents have thrown for hundreds of my very closest friends.

"Rosie," my dad whispered urgently, "I don't think—"

Mom was still looking at me encouragingly, happily, totally oblivious to how I was feeling.

I cleared my throat and grabbed the mic. I looked out at the sea of faces.

"Thanks, everyone, for coming to this party." There was an awkward silence. "It was a total and complete surprise, as you can see by the way I'm dressed!" Laughter. Laughter is good.

"I know this party is pretty over the top, but I want to thank my mom and dad and my brother for doing all this, for making it all so special." I managed a smile at all of them. I even meant what I said. As an experienced party-planner helper, I knew this had been an incredible amount of work. And they did it all without me suspecting a thing. "Even if Dad and 'Ro lied to me to get me to come here." Laughter again.

I gave the crowd a nervous smile, flicked off the mic, fumbled to put it back in its stand and bolted down the three steps. Mom had lit the candles on a table-sized cake set on a trolley. She wheeled it around to the front of the platform and held out her hand to me.

"*Happy birthday to you . . .*" she started singing and made a "c'mon, EVERYONE" gesture, throwing out her arms. Everyone else joined in, which is pretty much obligatory for "Happy Birthday." The kids sang in that half-hearted, half-embarrassed way that sixth graders do when they have to sing "Happy Birthday." But there were enough adults to carry the tune.

I gritted my teeth and stared down at my feet while a large room of people I didn't know sang for me. Some people want to be the center of attention. They crave it. They *long* for it. I know for a fact that Mom would have been happy to talk for hours up there with the mic. This was always astonishing to me. Even during the plays I'd been in, even behind the shield of a costume and a character, I never really wanted to be the center of attention. I never wanted to be the lead. I just wanted to be part of something.

All I wanted right now was for the bright, blinding glare of attention to shift far, far away from me. I'd never really realized how long and agonizingly slow "Happy Birthday" is, especially when it's led by a small woman who is determined to sing the extended clapping version. *"For she's a jolly good fellow . . . which nobody can deny"* and *"so say all of us!"* I don't even know if those were official "Happy Birthday" song verses, but Mom had everyone sing every one of them.

My smile was wavering into a sickly grimace when it finally, *finally* ended. It was such a complete and total relief when it was over and everyone focused their attention on the cake. Bless that attention-shifting cake. It really was a lovely cake—white icing with a beautiful pattern of silver and gold leaves framing my name.

As I looked at the huge cake with the twelve candles on it, a thought struck me.

"Do not even *think* about mentioning anything about *boyfriends* when I blow out these candles," I hissed in Mom's ear. "Not one word."

"Well, you know the rules: if one stays lit—" She broke off when she saw my face. "Okay, okay, Princess. I promise I won't embarrass you."

I don't trust you anymore, Mom. I'm sorry, but after this party, how could I?

I took a huge breath and blew out each and every candle, just to make sure.

☆ ☆ ☆

Mom and Dad started cutting the cake and handing it out to the kids who were lining up for a piece. I tried to help, to make myself useful, but Mom shooed me away.

"We got this, Diva, honey. I'm doing cake; Dad's got the plates and serviettes. You can't work on your birthday!"

"It's not actually my birthday," I muttered, shoving my hands in my pockets.

"Off you go! Mingle with your guests."

Right. Mingle.

I turned and looked uncertainly at the snaking lineup of kids—most of them were in groups, talking and laughing. I stood for a few minutes, hesitating, wishing I had my backpack to rummage in so I wasn't just standing there awkwardly.

"Hey, Deev." Dad nudged my arm, handing me a piece of cake. "First piece!" His eyes said "Please be having fun, please understand we did all this for you, please don't be mad."

"Thanks, Dad," I said, and found a smile for him. At least holding the plate of cake gave me something to do with my hands.

I bravely set out to mingle with my guests. I wandered down the lineup, but everyone seemed to be talking with somebody else. My mingling efforts lasted about thirty seconds before I realized that they were pointless. Short of mingling by force, by butting right into a group, there was no chance to mingle. I wasn't a mingler. There was nobody to mingle with. There would be no mingling.

I stood uncertainly, holding my cake, feeling increasingly desperate. Then I thought that maybe I could just go back and hide in that spot behind the speaker and wait there quietly until the party was over. I ducked behind the DJ platform, down the side wall of the room, and found my way back to my seat in the shadows behind the speaker.

I heard snippets of conversation from the people in line as I moved to the back of the room.

". . . I got a stuffie, and *these* and *these* from those DJ scrambles . . ."

". . . score! I won a real football. I thought the prizes were going to be lame . . ."

". . . this picture, no wait, *this* one is hilarious . . ."

". . . you weren't supposed to *keep* the mustache . . ."

". . . what is this thing? Is it an eraser? Do you eat it? No seriously, it smells good . . ."

". . . already had, like, four of those candy shish kebab things. And cotton candy. But that cake looks so delicious. I'm gonna be so sick . . ."

". . . yeah, my mom made me come, too. Whatever. I wasn't doing anything else . . ."

". . . shut *up*. That song is, like, my fav!"

". . . vanilla? You think vanilla? I'm betting chocolate. Hard to tell by the icing."

". . . which just made me want to *throw up* . . ."

I found my chair behind the speaker, dragged it a little deeper into the shadows, and put my plate of untasted cake on the floor beside me. I had no appetite at all; my stomach was a tight ball. I wished I hadn't heard that comment about somebody's mom making them come. At least two somebodys actually, because the person had said "my mom made me come, too." Also. More than one person had been forced to come to my party.

I sat with my elbows on my knees, staring at the floor between my feet. There was a popped balloon down there, a shriveled gold mess tied to a broken, frayed gold ribbon. I tried not to think about how it seemed like a symbol of this whole party.

The DJ was taking a break, maybe getting a piece of cake, so for the moment, the speakers were mercifully quiet.

But maybe the quiet wasn't such a good thing. Because a group of people stopped on the other side of the speaker in front of me, and I heard them very clearly.

And I wished I hadn't.

"So that's it for our list of *decent* music suggestions." I heard that voice every day at the back of class, talking to Kallie. It was Miko. "Twenty-seven songs. Should we just give it to the DJ and say his music sucks, or what?"

I stayed very still.

"Just put it on his DJ chair thingy. Anybody want to get cake?" I recognized Kallie's loud voice.

"I'd get some, but her mom is going to be all 'Miranda! Thank you for *coming!*' Like I had a choice. She seems to think I'm actually her kid's best friend or something. As if."

Shut up, Miranda. No she doesn't. She thinks you're insecure. But I know you're just mean.

"*I* want cake," grumbled Kallie. "She's giving out *monster* pieces . . ."

"Then go get some already! I'm just here for the loot bags," said Miko.

Excellent. Love you too, Miko.

"Me too," said Miranda. "It was right there on the invitation. No presents and 'awesome' loot bags. My dad said that sounded like a sweet deal—you don't need to *bring* anything, but you *get* something."

Your dad sounds like a super-great guy, Miranda. A real gentleman. My dad would never talk like that.

"Let's go put this list where the DJ can see it so he stops

playing that totally lame music," said Miranda. "And I want some of those balloons for my room."

"Just rip a bunch off the wall. Nobody's going to say anything."

"Let's check out that photo booth while everyone's swarming around the cake."

"But I want some caaake," wailed Kallie, her voice getting fainter as she trailed off after the others.

I sat very still and stared down at that popped balloon until I was sure they were gone.

That was not totally a bad thing, I told myself. Bad, but not *totally* bad. Yes, those girls are jerks, and yes, they're just here because (a) they have to be, and (b) they want stuff. But I hadn't been thinking that they came because they liked me or wanted to be my friend anyway.

Their conversation told me one thing that made me feel better. At least now I knew the invitations to this party said not to bring gifts, which was a huge relief. That made us seem way less horrible as a family—at least nobody could say we only had this huge party so we could cash in on a hundred and fifty presents. So—Mom, Dad—good call on that "no gifts" policy.

I couldn't imagine what kids would have brought, anyway. What do you bring a kid you don't know at all? Maybe the sort of stuff you get a teacher when you know nothing about their personal life. Mugs, gift cards, bubble bath. Maybe chocolates?

Wow, a huge pile of those I-don't-know-you-at-all kinds of gifts would have been truly depressing.

I suddenly felt very, very tired.

That feeling of being done. Crumpled up. Deflated. Just like a popped balloon.

CHAPTER 17

And That's (Finally) a Wrap, Folks

The DJ played a few more songs before he signed off with a "Later, sixth graders!" I didn't know if those were songs off Miko and Miranda's list, and I didn't care. The cotton candy man had long since wheeled his sugar-sticky cart out the door, the fake-grass putting green was rolled up, and there were people packing up the other stations. The regular room lights had been flicked on, and many of the kids had already left, grabbing loot bags from a side table as they went.

"Jeez, these loot bags are incredible," said a boy I recognized from another class as he dug in his shopping-bag-sized bag and pulled out a nerf football. "There's a massive lollipop, a writing journal, *gift card . . .*"

My mom must have stayed up nights stuffing all those. The thought of that made me feel so guilty.

I watched kids leave for a while, then stood up.

My eye fell on my piece of cake. I should probably at least taste it, I thought, but I just couldn't. I chucked it in the nearest garbage can and went to help clean up.

Spencer, Jeremy, and Shaya were just leaving by the far door. Shaya caught my eye and waved her cotton candy at me.

"Happy birthday!" she called from the door. "I tried to *find* you! Where you been? Thanks for the awesome party!"

Spencer and Jeremy turned, smiled, and waved.

"Thanks for coming," I called, and waved back.

Why, oh *why* hadn't I come out of hiding sooner? Three friendly people, three potential friends, there all along. And I'd been wasting my time listening to the mean ones.

Speaking of mean, there was Miranda, leaning against a wall, texting. Her mother and my mother were sitting at a table. Mrs. Clay was talking, and my mom looked sorry for her. She nodded, then shook her head sadly, then patted Mrs. Clay's hand.

Miranda shoved her phone in her back pocket, sighed theatrically, and pushed herself away from the wall. "*Mom*," she said, "Can we *go* already?"

"Okay, okay." Miranda's mother pushed her chair back. I saw her quickly reach up and wipe her eyes. Mom stood up with her, and put her arm around Mrs. Clay, giving her shoulders a little squeeze. Surprisingly, Mrs. Clay turned, smiled, and gave Mom a hug.

"Thanks, Rosie. Thanks for everything," she said. She saw me hovering and said brightly, "Hey, happy birthday, Diva. Awesome party, huh? Your folks did just an awesome job." Her smile was wobbly and watery.

"*Awe*some," echoed Miranda. And the look she gave me left no doubt that she was being totally sarcastic.

"Yeah, sure was," I said fake-cheerfully. Hey, you have to try. "Total surprise."

"I can believe it. Nobody would wear what you're wearing if they knew they were going to a party." She said this in a lowered voice so our mothers didn't hear it.

"Did you get a loot bag, Miranda?" Mom asked. "Can't leave without some loot!"

"Yeah. I took one for my sister, too. That's okay, right? And some balloons." Miranda nodded her head to where some gold balloons were tied to two loot bags. She clearly wasn't the slightest bit interested in whether it was okay with Mom. She wasn't asking for permission at all. She'd already pulled out her phone and was looking down at it.

"Of course, of course." Mom smiled until they left. Then she turned to me and said: "Her sister is eighteen and doesn't even live at home anymore. Ah, well, such a sad family. In fact, Julie and her husband are splitting up. Anyway, we can be generous."

"Yeah, I guess."

I was amazed that Mom knew all that about Miranda's family. All of that was *way* worse than being a party mermaid or having to play the Yellow Brick Road. It didn't make Miranda any nicer. It didn't erase the meanness. But maybe it *explained* her just a little.

I turned to help Dad and 'Ro pull all the silver streamers down.

Most of the gold balloons were already popped or gone.

☆ ☆ ☆

It was almost eleven o'clock when we got home. My legs were cramped from our seats being pushed as far forward as they could go so we could fit all the totes in the back. Mom and Dad both looked as exhausted as I felt. It was only 'Ro who still seemed to have lots of energy. Way too much. Hyperdrive energy. He was nattering about the "rules" of balloon volleyball all the way home.

"'Ro! There *are* no rules. It's just made up. It's not a real sport," I said irritably.

"Oh, so you can let the balloon hit the *floor*? You can hit it *under* the net? *Kick it*?" He rolled his eyes at my seemingly incredible stupidity. "Of course there are rules. And that Simon hit it against the wall, which can't be right, because what sport lets you use a wall . . ."

"Too much sugar," Dad muttered. He saluted Gary the Centaur like he always did as he pulled the van into the garage.

"We're leaving all this stuff *right here*," Mom said through a huge yawn. "We can unpack tomorrow. After we sleep in. Late."

"Well, thanks everybody. Great party. I'm heading off to bed." I could barely see straight I was so tired. It was exhaustion mixed with a kind of weak-kneed gratitude that I wouldn't have to deal with anything like that again for at least a year. And if I could figure out how to actually get through to Mom, possibly never again.

"Love you, Princess! Happy birthday!"

"Love you."

"I'm coming up with you, Deev," said 'Ro quickly, appearing by my side. He peered up the dark staircase. "Creepy up there."

I switched on all the lights in the hall, in the bathroom, and in both our bedrooms. 'Ro did a quick scan of his room, a casual glance under his bed and in his closet.

"It's so late and dark that I think we should keep our doors open tonight, Deev, and maybe the hall light on. Might help you sleep."

"Yeah, good idea, thanks 'Ro." *Did this little tough guy really think he was fooling me?*

I pushed my door wide open after I'd changed and brushed my teeth.

"Goodnight, 'Ro!" I called.

"'Night," he called back, his voice sounding very little.

I'd crawled into bed, turned onto my side, and was just drifting off when I saw a little silhouette in my doorway.

"Mmmff, what's up, 'Ro?"

"I was just thinking you might want me to sleep in *here* tonight. Just tonight. Because you might be feeling weird from the party. You know, lots of noise and people, and it's so late and creepy and *dark*. I could just sleep on the floor right here beside your bed or something. If you wanted."

"That's nice of you. Good idea, but you better hop in here." I threw open the duvet on the far side of my double bed. "It's chilly, and I don't have other blankets."

He scrambled in over me before I even finished the sentence and snuggled down by the wall.

"I'll stay on my side."

"Yeah, you better."

"You won't even know I'm here," he said.

The bed lurched for a ridiculous amount of time as 'Ro thrashed around, getting comfortable. So much for me not knowing he was there.

Finally, he settled, and gave a big sigh.

Silence.

"Deev?" 'Ro had the loudest whisper of anyone I'd ever known. It was louder than many people's speaking voices. I sighed.

"*What,* 'Ro?"

"You didn't like the party, did you?"

How was I supposed to answer that? With a lie, of course.

"The party?" I said, stalling. "Of course I liked it. It was pretty amazing."

"Dad said you wouldn't want something so big, but me and Mom thought you would. We thought it would be fun. We two-against-one'd him. But he was right, wasn't he?"

I turned onto my back, staring up through the gloom at the shadowy pattern the trees threw onto the ceiling.

"'Ro, it was a great party, and I totally appreciate the work you and Mom and Dad must have put into it. It's just that there were a lot of people I didn't know there, right? So."

"Yeah, and some of them were *jerks*," said 'Ro loudly. "That one girl kept throwing candy on the floor. And that guy that said the music "sucked"—right out loud instead of just thinking it. And that other boy that cheated at balloon volleyball. And Miranda tore down those balloons to take home without even asking Mom or Dad, and she took *two* loot bags and I saw her take one of the mustaches!"

"What *will* we ever do without that mustache?" I said, trying to keep a straight face.

"It's not funny. It's stealing."

"I know. You're right, Officer Pankowksi. But I guess if you get that many people together, there's bound to be some jerks, right? But some good people, too. Some nice ones." And there were nice people at the party, I remembered. Some really nice people.

"I guess."

"You guys made my birthday really special, 'Ro. I'll never forget that party, right?" I was trying to be honest. I really would never, ever forget that party. "But you know, 'Ro, Dad and I are different from you and Mom. We're quieter. Lower key. Not so great with people. Not so over the top."

"More *under*-the-top," said 'Ro.

I laughed. "Exactly. So under-the-top we're almost *burrowing*."

"That's okay," said 'Ro. "Lots of things burrow. Worms. Bugs. Moles . . ."

"Wow, feeling *way* better over here," I said.

"I just mean that one way isn't right and another way isn't wrong," said 'Ro. "It's not *wrong* for a mole to burrow because that's what it *does*. That's its mole instinct."

"Gotcha. You're right. The old mole instinct. Okay, it's sooo late."

Silence.

"I'm super-tired," yawned 'Ro.

"Finally," I said. "'Night, 'Ro."

"'Night, mole."

I smiled up into the darkness.

CHAPTER 18

The Yellow Brick Road Reveal

If I'd had the choice between going to school on Monday and, say, swimming with sharks, I might honestly have picked the sharks. I didn't know if people were going to gossip about *DIVAPALOOZA!*, think I was a spoiled brat, or just go back to forgetting all about me. I was hoping for a little invisibility.

"So that's the last one," I said, puffing from loading four bags of sandbox sand into the van. Mom had a Gold Rush kids' party this week, and the highlight was the panning for gold-foil-covered chocolate coins in a huge tub of sand. It used to be gold beads in kitty litter, until I pointed out how completely gross that was.

"Thanks so much, kiddo. The gold-panning is always a *huge* hit with the little ones. I've even spray-painted these." She held out a handful of fake gold nuggets. They looked surprisingly realistic. "They'll love them. So that's Tuesday." She closed her eyes to think. "Then Thursday night is the 'Old Hollywood Glamour Party' (I've got streamers made of feather boas!), then Saturday afternoon is that 'Bucket List Bash.'"

"So, slow week," I said. "Wait, what's a 'Bucket List Bash'?"

"Oh, it's for a couple who are revealing their bucket list for their retirement! You know, what they want to do, where they want to go, that sort of thing."

"And they're having a party. For that?"

"Why not?" Mom laughed. "Can't ever have too many parties, right? I've got a beautiful chalkboard easel that I'm going to stand in two buckets! Get it? *Bucket* list. And they'll write out the list with colored chalk after the slide show . . ."

She talked as we stacked totes. She was creative, I had to hand it to her. Creative with endlessly exhausting energy. The Pink Palace Party Planners was obviously doing very well. She was excitedly telling me about a new theme party that was getting lots of interest.

"It's called 'Matrimania'! (with an exclamation point!). It's sort of a huge kickoff party to start the planning of a wedding."

Seriously. To *start* all the engagement parties and showers and bridal weekends and all the other hoopla that was apparently mandatory when people got married. All of which never made any sense to me. Why did I always feel like a total alien when we talked parties?

"So, how about you?" Mom said. "What's on this week?" Her voice was bright, but her face looked anxious. I think Mom knew that *DIVAPALOOZA!* hadn't been the slam-dunk success she'd been hoping for. Or maybe she still hoped that somehow the party would change things for me at school, get all those sixth graders talking about the new girl, have people running up to me, begging to be friends.

Either way, we hadn't talked about it. I'd barely set foot outside my room all Saturday.

"Me? Oh, just school. And rehearsals for the play start up this week . . ." I was regretting ever auditioning for the play and dreading our first rehearsal after school tomorrow. That's when the whole Yellow Brick Road role would go from being a small, baffling private embarrassment to a full-blown public humiliation.

"I'm sure it'll go better than you think," Mom said. "I'm sure of it."

"Well, I couldn't imagine it going worse than I think it's going to go," I joked.

But I wasn't really joking.

☆ ☆ ☆

I was so nervous about the rehearsal on Monday, I'd barely eaten all day.

And now I was a cold-handed, tight-stomached, thumping-hearted mess. I jumped a mile when the dismissal bell rang, even though I'd been watching the clock through all of Science.

I shoved everything into my backpack and headed for the theater. There were already a lot of kids in the hall waiting outside the doors.

"Locked?" Spencer wandered down the hall and stood beside me, craning to see why we were stalled. "She's usually a little late. Hey, fun birthday party on Friday! I can't believe I almost ruined the surprise."

"Hi, guys. What surprise?" Shaya asked, dumping her backpack on the ground.

"I almost said to Diva 'See you at the party' when we were talking in class on Friday. *So* stupid. I couldn't believe I almost ruined the surprise. Me! Who loves surprise parties more than me? I didn't, did I? Ruin it?" He looked at me anxiously.

Aahhh, so *that* was why he had flushed and run away. It was a huge relief that it hadn't been my special brand of friend-repellent.

"Haha. No, no, you didn't ruin it. Not at all. It was a *total* surprise, believe me."

"Which is a total *miracle*, actually," said Shaya. "With the whole grade there." I looked at her quickly, sensing criticism, but the look she gave me back was open and friendly. She was just stating a fact. The whole grade *had* been there, whether I had wanted them there or not.

"Yeah, my mom tends to do things in a big way. *Really* big. Always over the top."

"That's fun, right?" Shaya asked. She saw the expression on my face. "Or possibly, sometimes it could really suck." I laughed. She nailed it.

"Your mom's so nice," said Spencer. "Gave me an extra-ginormous piece of cake!"

Thank you, Mom.

"Your parents did an awesome job," said Shaya. "It was an incredible party. Like, I've never been to a party with so much fun stuff to do!"

"Thanks. I'll let them know you said that. It'll mean a lot to Mom especially."

My heart was beating so fast. A conversation, that's what I was having. A real, normal conversation. With real, normal people who seemed to be becoming friends. I was grateful they didn't ask where I'd been the whole party. Pretty tricky making that lonely seat behind the speaker sound fun. Or anything other than pathetic.

"Oh, good. Here's Madame Ducharme," said Spencer. The crowd of kids moved aside so she could unlock the door.

"Okay, okay, so much noise! Quiet yourselves. Find a seat.

Sit, sit down!" she called. "You will all be the audience for the moment!"

"Follow me, Diva!" Shaya yelled, elbowing and pushing her way expertly through the crush of kids streaming into the theater. I followed her bobbing curly head as she weaved through the crowd.

"Wow, you are *good* at that," I said as we snatched two seats together.

She shrugged and smiled.

"I have three brothers."

Madame Ducharme climbed the steps and walked to center stage. Her heels tapped loudly as she walked. The acoustics in the theater were so good you could even hear the jangle of her necklaces and bracelets.

"So. This is the first time St. George"—she pronounced it "Sant Jhorzh"—"will present *The Wizard of Oz*. You have seen the old film? Many of you are, perhaps, familiar with this story, yes?"

Most of the kids nodded or said yes.

"Well—" she snapped her fingers "—forget all that you think you know. This production will be nothing like that. *Nothing*. No little dogs. No silly voices. No slapstick jokes." She threw out her arm theatrically. "It will be *modern*. Black and white. *Stark*. I see mirrors, glass, shadows, light." She let her arm drift down.

There was dead silence in the room. I wondered if anybody else was getting a very bad feeling about this.

Miranda raised her hand.

"I still get to wear the ruby sequined shoes, right? Because my mom already bought the costume." I noticed Miranda always phrased questions so that she got the answer she wanted.

A ripple of annoyance passed over Madame Ducharme's face.

"Ah, those ruby-red shoes. We can never be rid of those," she muttered. "Well, if it is done, of course you can wear them. They are iconic after all. But no other bright color, I forbid it. Scarecrow: beige. Tin Man: silver. Lion: tan. No *real* color until Emerald City. Then, the production will *explode* with color!"

She looked out at the silent audience.

"No. That is not right. I just lied to you. There will be one more bright color, only *one* other than the ruby-red shoes—" she closed her eyes as if in pain "—until the riot of color in Emerald City. And that color is . . . *yellow*. Yellow. Yellow for hope, for longing, for *life*."

I scrunched down in my seat.

"The Yellow Brick Road, of course, played by our little Diva! Where is Diva?" Madame Ducharme shielded her eyes with her hand and searched the crowd. Kids turned around to look as well.

"Uh, Diva?" Shaya whispered, giving me a nudge with a sharp elbow.

I put up my hand.

"Ah, *there* she is." Madame Ducharme gestured to me. My

ears were pulsing hot, my face burning. I stared down at my hands gripping each other in my lap.

Madame Ducharme paused. Did she actually want me to say something? What? I still didn't know what the ridiculous role *meant*. I didn't have a clue what I was supposed to *do*. Panic blotted out anything I might have thought of saying.

"When I saw that on the cast list, I thought it was a joke," Miranda said, filling the silence with her loud voice. "I mean, it's just some kind of prop, right? The Yellow Brick Road can't be some sort of weird *character* . . ."

"Mmm . . . more of a *presence*," said Madame Ducharme mysteriously. A presence? A *presence*? How was I supposed to act like a "presence"? What did that even mean? Was that like a ghost?

"So," she continued, "imagine: Dorothy has been swept up in the tornado. A force of nature! Wind. Noise. Drama." She made swirling motions with her hands. "Then: a loud *CRASH* as the farmhouse plummets to the earth! A blood-curdling SHRIEK as the Wicked Witch of the East is crushed! Dorothy emerges into a dark and desolate place. Then: joy, jubilation! The Munchkin people (who in this production will *not* be annoying or speak in silly voices) celebrate the death of the tyrant-dictator, and the spirit of their nation's revolution!"

Madame Ducharme was clearly taking a few liberties with the script.

"Revolution?" said Miranda. "What revolution?

"Yes, yes. *Revolution.* It is their day of independence from tyranny! The song 'Ding-Dong! The Witch Is Dead' becomes an anthem for their new country, for freedom, for the revolt against oppression. Dorothy marches with them in solidarity. End of scene!"

I was going to have to study this script, because I felt like I knew nothing about this play.

Madame Ducharme paused dramatically.

"Then, the stage, it is completely dark. Still. Then: SPOT-LIGHT! What is that? Something moves! It is a long, flowing yellow robe that is a *road* that gathers itself up, and then—"

"—then I'll sing 'Follow the Yellow Brick Road,'" interrupted Miranda excitedly. "I've been practicing that one. It's one of the show's best songs!"

"No. Not you, Dorothy. The *Yellow Brick Road* itself sings the song," Madame Ducharme said triumphantly. She pointed at me. "The *Road* sings the song! Beckoning them to follow. Diva's unusual, husky, low voice is perfect for the suggestion of mystery, enchantment. Following the Yellow Brick Road will be a symbol of taking a leap into the great unknown!"

A few kids turned to glance uncertainly at me. Miranda threw me a hostile glance, the smile she kept on her face for Madame Ducharme dropping like a stone.

"But I think *Dorothy* should sing that song," she protested. She was so angry her voice was shaking. "It's all about *her.*"

"Not in this production," Madame Ducharme said in a brisk voice. Miranda sat back in her seat and crossed her arms, a mottled flush spreading over her face and neck. I felt sick to my stomach. None of this was my fault, but it was a pretty sure bet that Miranda would take this out on me. What would a furious Miranda be like? I didn't even want to know.

"There will be plenty of singing for Dorothy," the director said. "Many, many songs for your beautiful voice to sing, Miranda. Now. I will go into greater detail . . ."

I relaxed a bit now that the attention wasn't centered on me and settled in to listen to the rest of Madame Ducharme's vision for the play. She made it a bit of a performance—a one-person show. She may be directing this play, but she was an actor at heart.

This was going to be different than any other play I'd ever been in. And while I was still unsure about it, I found myself more and more interested in my part. And as Madame Ducharme talked and shouted and explained and gestured, I felt it—in me, in the rest of the kids, sizzling through the whole theater.

That feeling of excitement when you're part of a group doing something new and thrilling and big.

CHAPTER 19

Nowhere to Hide

I t's one thing to have Madame Ducharme set out her great, exciting vision for the play. But it's a whole other thing to have to lie on the dusty stage floor during rehearsals pretending to be a magical road with some kind of "presence."

I kept telling myself it would get better when Mom had finished my costume and I had something to hide behind. I made sure Mom talked to Madame Ducharme so she knew what to make. She came home from the parents' meeting very excited about the "vision" for my role, hauling in acres of yellow material from the fabric store down to her sewing machine.

"It's going to be phe*nom*enal, Deev! An a*maz*ing costume!"

I scrambled down the stairs after her.

"I'm going to be able to walk in it, right, Mom? Because that's super-important. There are stairs up and down the sides of the stage, and I have to move from side to side when I'm onstage. I also have a lot of turns. It won't be tight at the ankles like the mermaid tail?"

"Oh, no. Long, loose. *Flowing.*"

I relaxed.

"What an inspiring lady Madame Ducharme is," Mom said. "This production is going to be so big, so lavish, you could be performing it on *Broadway*! And I joined the parent committee doing the sets!" she said. "We're doing exciting things with long mirrors and mirrored tile. They're supposed to 'reflect the audience back at themselves.' At least, I think that's what Madame Ducharme said. Something like that. Poetical. Anyway, it'll sure be a sparkly show!"

As I listened to her, I had a cowardly yearning for the slapped-together plays at my old school. Where kids stayed in at lunch recess painting messy sets on cardboard refrigerator boxes the custodian hauled from an appliance shop. Where people used old Halloween costumes and dress-up clothes for their parts. For example, Warren Pitts just wore a big, yellow mustache (that he had to keep pressing back onto his upper lip) and a long, fuzzy orange sweater as his costume for the Lorax. At my old school, kids forgot their lines and it was no big deal because somebody else just helped them with a few whispered words until they caught the thread again.

Yes, those plays were lame. Thrown together. Small-time.

Probably very, very painful to watch. But at least they'd been fun. They'd been *ours*. And, more important, they were almost stress-free. Zero pressure.

I was already stomach-churningly nervous about this gala production. Warren Pitts would never have gotten a lead role in this school play, and if he did (by some miracle), he'd have been stuffed into an expensive, professional-grade, orange fake fur Lorax onesie before you could say "Truffula Tree."

The number of people involved in this *Wizard of Oz* play was daunting. There were almost seventy kids performing, another group of Tech Club kids working the theater's complicated sound and lights system, a team of hyper-perfectionist parents doing sets and costumes, and several teachers assisting Madame Ducharme. Mom was right. A big, over-the-top, Broadway-scale production. And there was very little laughing or joking around during rehearsals. It was all business once we had each gotten a full script of the play.

"Know the whole play, but especially you must know your own *role*. Back to front. Up and down," said Madame Ducharme firmly. "I will 'ave no patience for people forgetting their lines. Learn them. Recite them. Word by word by word."

On paper, The Yellow Brick Road wasn't such a bad part. I only had to sing the "Follow the Yellow Brick Road" song, which I knew already and, even if I didn't, was so simple and mindlessly repetitive that I'd have to have been a total slacker not to be able to memorize it pretty quickly. Not exactly rocket science. I had other lines, too, but not many. The Road wasn't much of a talker.

But because I was onstage during Dorothy meeting the Scarecrow, the Tin Man, and the Lion, basically leading them all the way to Emerald City, there were a lot of stage directions for my part. Where I was supposed to be, whether I swept the road left or right, and which side of the stage I exited. Lots of stuff I had to remember. I honestly didn't know if I could do it the way Madame Ducharme wanted it done. I hoped she wouldn't be disappointed in me.

But the real problem, the *huge* problem, with my role was that I was onstage with Miranda all the time. Or, as she probably saw it, *she* was onstage, but I had to be there, too.

I have to be honest, though. Miranda was an amazing Dorothy. It pains me to say it, because meanly, secretly, I hoped she wouldn't be. But she is a born actress, completely losing herself in the role, so that at times you really, truly believed she *was* Dorothy, swept up in a tornado and desperate to find her way home. I liked Miranda waaaay better when she was Dorothy.

And her *voice*. When she sang, everyone in the theater went still and silent and just listened. Crystal clear, beautiful, and so alive. It gave me goosebumps. It was as if her flat, dead, daytime, non-theater voice belonged to somebody else, as if she were saving up all the emotion for her Dorothy voice. As if she were two separate people.

But rehearsal after rehearsal, I came to realize that theater-Miranda wasn't completely different than regular-Miranda. In the midst of a big production where we were all supposed to work together, she was still astonishingly selfish. She threw herself into her role, sure, but when she wasn't actually talking or singing, she resented not being the center of attention.

Especially when I was. She did not want me there, and she let me know it.

She started out with small acts of sabotage. She would look away as if completely bored, and fidget or pick at her nails. I was too busy flushing and singing and stammering out my lines to care, but I started to notice her when I calmed down. Then her distractions became bigger: she'd sigh or hum or swing her arms or pretend to be practicing a few dance steps. Just enough so that I got thrown off the rhythm of the song or lost the train of my lines.

She really took it up a notch during my only solo song—"Follow the Yellow Brick Road." It became a total nightmare. I guess Miranda was still bitter that I "stole" her song, as she so inaccurately hissed at me during one rehearsal. She hummed "Somewhere Over the Rainbow" all the way through *my* song, just loud enough for me to hear, but not so loud that Madame Ducharme, sitting in the stalls, could hear. I had to frantically block out the humming while trying to sing. I tried to ignore her, but it was almost impossible.

Miranda watched me like a hawk. If I wasn't *exactly* where I was supposed to be (or, sometimes, even if I was), she'd stop everything, call me out, and make a big deal of it. She'd groan in frustration and snap: "Road is supposed to be stage left!" Or "Road is in my way!" Or "How can I dance with Road right here?"

Never "Diva." Never even "you" or "she." Always "Road." Or "It." Not a person, not a human being. Deliberately. I knew it was pathetic, it was *so* pathetic, but it still bothered me. A lot.

Today's rehearsal was especially, particularly dismal. Miko (who was the Tin Man. No heart; pretty accurate) and Kallie (the Scarecrow. No brain; accurate again) were onstage with Miranda and me when Caleb shuffled in from stage right. He was the Cowardly Lion and was actually really funny in the role.

"Who . . . who . . ." he started his lines, cringing comically and jumping away from us in fear, landing with a big thump.

A wooden tree prop near me wobbled and fell backward from the impact. I tried to catch it as it fell but missed.

"Oh my God!" Miranda stopped everything. "Road is so *clumsy*!" she wailed over to Madame Ducharme. "It's throwing all of us off!"

"She didn't—" Caleb started to say.

"Shut up," hissed Miranda.

"Remind me again why Road is here at all, Professor," she

called angrily. "This scene, *every* scene actually, would be better without Road. We could just find some yellow carpet or something."

"You would like to be the director, too, Miranda?" Madame Ducharme sighed. "Calm, people, calm. We all work together. Miranda, a little less drama; Diva, perhaps a little more carefulness? There, it is *over*."

My face felt hot. It wasn't worth complaining. Madame Ducharme wouldn't believe me.

I looked at Miranda. Her angry, triumphant eyes glared back.

It's not over, I thought.

And it wasn't.

☆ ☆ ☆

Miranda continued her covert sabotage. She'd shoulder me out of the way, even though I was where I was supposed to be. If I struggled with a line, I'd look up and she'd be looking at me with a smirk. She'd sigh when I started singing, and hum through the song. She took to lightly tapping her ruby-red slipper to throw me off the beat.

And she did all these things when no one else was close enough to hear. Only she and I knew she was doing it.

And that's the thing about being onstage with someone. Or, I guess, being bullied generally.

There's nowhere to hide.

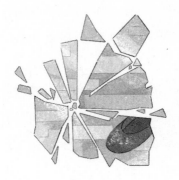

CHAPTER 20

A Smash Hit (Literally)

The rehearsals went on. And on and on and on.

They went on to the point where, as Shaya said, "I will seriously throw up if I ever have to watch this show again. Like *ever*. In my whole, entire life."

We were eating our lunches outside under my tree. My days of backpack rummaging were gone. Shaya and I were officially friends and ate our lunches under the tree every day. Jeremy and Spencer often came by as well.

"Honestly," she said, "I'm one of like a *thousand* Munchkins. I run in holding up my sign and yell a bit with all of them about our Munchkin revolution. We're onstage for three, four minutes. Then it's over and I have to watch the rest of the play for the millionth time."

I knew how she felt. I was desperate for the play to be over and done with. I hadn't told her about Miranda wrecking every scene for me. I hadn't told anyone. It would all have sounded so pathetic and small: "So this girl clears her throat or taps her ruby-red shoe when I'm just starting to sing. And sometimes she totally ignores me, but sometimes she stares at me hard and even smiles a little! And she knows and I know—only the two of us know—that she's being mean, and that I feel trapped and helpless. And she knows I dread being up there with her, and it gets worse when I give her any reaction at all, and it never, ever stops . . ."

Who would believe that? Who would believe mind games like that? I probably wouldn't if it wasn't actually happening to me.

Anyway, rehearsals intensified the week before the show—three during the week and one on the weekend. Madame Ducharme was increasingly snappish and irritable, which made all the actors more on edge. The lighting in the theater short-circuited. A Munchkin twisted her ankle and had to go to the hospital for an x-ray. The girl with the really good scream (like, I'm talking horror-movie good screamer), whose only role was to be off-stage and scream when the farmhouse supposedly landed on the Wicked Witch of the East, lost her voice. You can only let loose so many blood-curdling screams, I guess, before the old throat shuts down. Anyway, a girl with a far inferior scream got put in the part. These things all seemed small, but the small things added up.

It seemed like the more we rehearsed the more problems happened. The play got worse, not better. Bumpier, not smoother.

Mercifully, May 28 finally came around. The night of the performance. The very, very end of the Yellow Brick Road.

Mom had made an incredible costume for me. It was a long, loose gown, almost like a ghost costume, only yellow. There was a round hole for my face, and slits for my arms, but otherwise, the costume trailed far behind me when I walked, like a long, long cape. She'd Sharpied the black outline of bricks all over the costume, bigger at the end of the cape, getting smaller as they got near my head.

"Perspective! See?" She'd shown me in the mirrors at home. It was a neat illusion: when my back was turned, when I was walking away from the audience, the road looked like it was receding into the distance.

I wore a yellow long-sleeved shirt and leggings underneath. And, because I begged for it, Mom found some yellow face paint online. I wanted to be almost completely invisible. No Diva, just Yellow Brick Road.

The cast was supposed to arrive at school an hour early. I decided to put on my costume at home because it involved a lot of struggling and material management. Mom helped me into the costume and did my face paint. She even bricked over my face with eyeliner.

"Wow," I said, for once grateful for those full-length mirrors by the stairs. "That looks great. You did an awesome job on this costume, Mom."

"Oh, good," she said, looking relieved. "I'm so happy you like it! I have a great—"

"No, no," I interrupted her, holding up a hand. "If it's a great feeling you have, I'm glad. Good. But just don't say it. No great feelings, Mom. No warm-fuzzies. Just tell me to break a leg. That's what actors tell each other."

"Break a leg, honey," she laughed. "You go break *both* of them."

Dad walked me over to the school, carrying the back of my long costume like a bridesmaid at a royal wedding. People stared out the window of a car that drove by, and I giggled at how ridiculous that weird, long yellow brick ghost and her helper must look.

"How you doing up there?" Dad called.

I turned my yellow face. "I'm okay. Nervous."

"Curb coming up. There you go. Me too, actually. I'm nervous too. It'll be fine. Fun!" Dad was trying very hard to be positive. Brave, even. I knew, though, that being in a play was the very last thing in the world he would choose to do. His nervousness was all for me.

As we passed Miranda's house, there was a burst of loud shouting. Then a door slammed. Hard.

I glanced over my shoulder at Dad. He shook his head and shrugged a little.

"Not a great situation there," he said in a low voice. "Not a happy house, Mom says."

We crossed the street to the school.

"I can take it from here, Dad," I said, once we were inside. "Thanks for the help."

"You sure? Dust bunnies down the hall . . ."

"This is St. George, Dad. No dust bunnies allowed."

"Haha. You look *great*. Very Yellow Brick Road-ish."

"Excellent."

We looked at each other. He ran a hand over his thinning hair. I could see him struggling for words.

"Almost over," he said. "Almost summer vacation, Deev. Then you can relax. You won't have to worry about a thing."

"Thanks, Dad."

"So, see you from the audience!"

"See you from the stage! I better get going here."

"Yep, you betcha. Get out of here." He gave me an awkward hug and pulled away with a smear of yellow face paint on his blue shirt. He gave a little wave and turned, walking quickly away.

I swooshed my way down to the theater.

☆ ☆ ☆

There is nothing quite like the opening night of a play. There should be a word for the feeling, although maybe there are too many things all going on at once for it to fit into just one word. I'll have to think about that for my book.

The actors are all in costume and makeup, and there's a backstage atmosphere of suppressed excitement and nervousness. Some people get quiet, some get loud, some get panicky, some get chatty, some get annoying. I was, not surprisingly, one of the quiet ones. The play, which seemed stale and boring at rehearsal yesterday, started to take on an exciting life of its own, and seemed fresh and new.

And there were the sounds from the other side of the curtain. Sounds of families and friends and students and teachers talking, laughing, coming in, settling down, taking their seats. There was a cheerful, expectant feeling in the audience, with maybe a little simmering nervousness thrown in.

I hiked up my costume and waddled over to the curtain where a bunch of other kids were peeking out at the audience. The theater was almost full of what seemed like an incredible number of people. I searched the crowd near the front, sure that my family would have come early to get good seats. Sure enough, there they were in the third row—Mom and Dad and Hero. Dad was still wearing the yellow-smeared shirt. Mom and Dad were holding hands, and both of them were laughing at something Hero was saying.

"My family is basically taking up the whole left side of the theater," whispered Shaya, giggling. She looked cute in her Munchkin costume, her dark hair curling out from under a colorful, floppy hat. "Honestly, my parents, my brothers, my grandparents, my aunt, my uncle, my cousins. I better make my three minutes count!"

Two sharp claps sounded behind us. Madame Ducharme's call to the cast to gather around her.

Before I turned away from the curtain, I saw Miranda's parents, a few rows behind my family. They were both dressed up—she was wearing a sparkly top, dangly earrings, and lots of makeup, and he was wearing a suit. She looked miserable and he had his arms crossed and an angry look on his face. In that laughing, chattering crowd, they sat in a bubble of dead silence, staring straight ahead at the black curtain.

☆ ☆ ☆

As the curtain rose, I had a moment of complete peace. There was nothing I could do about anything now, other than do my best. I knew my part, this whole play, better than I knew some parts of my pink house. Whatever happened, whatever this evening held, it would be over soon.

I watched the first scene from the wings. A huge burlap backdrop was the only set for the farm in Kansas. Everything went well, and Miranda did an amazing job of the last song—"Somewhere Over the Rainbow." I saw people in the audience wiping away tears and heard the thunderous applause as the curtain closed.

Second scene. The sound system played crashing sounds

of a destructive tornado. Dorothy staggered around the stage, making the wind from four fans offstage look like a straight-up terrifying storm. Then swirling lights and howling wind. The girl with the inferior scream managed her best one yet—a real ear-shatterer. Then the tech kids played the horrible crashing sound they'd taped, which I think was them banging on an empty dumpster with brooms. *That* had the audience jumping in their seats.

"Munchkin time," whispered Shaya, punching me on the shoulder as she passed me, trooping onto the stage with all the others, rallying around Dorothy. They sang a spirited version of "Ding-Dong! The Witch Is Dead."

My hands started to get clammy. It was almost time for me to go onstage.

Focus, Diva.

I listened closely to what was happening onstage, heart thumping, waiting for my cue.

"You, Dorothy of Kansas, are a great hero of our revolution! Long live Dorothy! Long live Munchkin Independence!" The Munchkin mob cheered.

Enter green and evil Wicked Witch of the West hunting for the ruby-red slippers, which appear as if by magic on Dorothy. She is enraged and vanishes with her trademark bloodcurdling cackle and vows of revenge. Glinda, the much-less-interesting good witch, directs Dorothy to seek out the great Wizard of Oz in Emerald City, who can help her find her way home.

"Follow the Yellow Brick Road, Dorothy. And remember: don't take off those magical red shoes." She clomped offstage. Despite Madame Ducharme's best efforts, our play's Glinda played this role like a cop.

"My, people come and go so quickly here," said a bewildered Dorothy.

"Come with us, we will take you to the Yellow Brick Road!" the Munchkins cried. And everyone talked excitedly as they walked off the stage. The curtains closed.

Showtime.

I ran onto the dark, empty stage as quickly as my enormous costume allowed. A teacher ran on and spread my cape out behind me. I lay down in position as another teacher whisked away the farm backdrop. My heart was pounding as I lay, cheek to the stage floor. I took a deep breath, then flattened my body as much as I could.

As the curtains opened, I heard the audience gasp and murmur. The stage set for this scene, for the rest of the play, was incredible—tall mirrors lined the back of the stage, set at angles from each other. Plexiglas "crystals" hung from the rafters. With the stage lights dazzling off the mirrors and the glass, the set was sparkling, icy, brilliant.

Then the cue from offstage. A Munchkin voice.

"There it is, Dorothy! There! The Yellow Brick Road!"

The spotlights danced crazily, then all converged on me. Dead silence in the theater.

You are a presence, I reminded myself. *You are the road to Home. You lead to all good things. You are important.*

I rose slowly, my back to the audience. I heard them murmuring excitedly behind me.

"Thank you! Oh, thank you so much!" Dorothy's voice came from offstage.

Now, rehearsal after rehearsal, Madame Ducharme emphasized that Dorothy was just supposed to *hurry* onto the stage. Not sprint. Just a purposeful fast-walk. Madame Ducharme told her this many, many, *many* times. "Slow down, Miranda," she'd say. "Slow. There is no race here."

Miranda argued that because Dorothy was so impatient to get home, she would have *run* toward the Yellow Brick Road. In rehearsals, though, she listened to Madame Ducharme.

But now, here was Miranda sprinting onto the stage in a blur of gingham and red braids. I heard the heels of the ruby-red shoes clicking, fast, fast, fast toward me. She was running quickly, swept up in the adrenalin of performing, in the exhilaration of being a star in front of an audience.

Then something happened.

I don't actually know what happened. She must have slipped or stumbled or tripped over her own feet. I saw her sprawl and fall in a spinning slide. I heard a muffled shriek from an offstage Munchkin and one of the parents in the front row shouted, "Whoa, look out!" And then Miranda crashed spectacularly into one of the tall mirrors at the back of the stage. Whatever happened, I was probably six feet away from her, so mercifully she couldn't blame me for any of it. Let's be honest, she probably still would, but whatever.

There was a breathless moment when she jumped back to her feet and staggered back from the mirror a few steps. The *mirror.* Both of us stared in horror at the mirror, at the snaking pattern of cracks that worked its way swiftly from the bottom crash site to the top. I had no idea mirrors would do that. It cracked like glass in a cartoon.

It only took seconds, but when the glass cracked to the top, there was a dramatic pause, as if the mirror was deciding what to do.

I lunged in and pulled Miranda away just as the mirror shattered down all over the stage behind us.

CHAPTER 21

Freedom Takes Center Stage

A few split seconds can hold a lot of thoughts:

Wow, I did not see that one coming.

What are we going to do?

Remember the Lorax, when Mrs. Krantz stepped in and saved the show.

It's not my problem. I didn't wreck this play.

Miranda looks confused. Scared. Little. Like she's going to faint. Or run right off this stage. Oh no, you don't, Miranda.

Step in, Diva. Step up.

Do something!

I took a deep breath and pulled Miranda to the front of the stage. The spotlights followed us.

We faced each other. She was breathing hard. She looked

shaken and uncertain. Over her shoulder in the wings, I saw Madame Ducharme giving frantic directions to her assistants.

"Your world is broken," I improvised, spreading the cape of my costume out with my arms to try to shield the two teachers who had crept onto the stage behind us to sweep up the mirror shards. "That is true. So true. It is shattered and confused. But do not lose heart. There is a way forward, a way that leads out of here. Follow me. Follow the Yellow Brick Road."

I started to sing "Follow the Yellow Brick Road." My voice felt strong, steady. I was a presence. It was just me and my voice and the spotlight.

I wasn't even annoyed when Miranda lifted up her chin and started singing, too. I was actually glad. Our duet was actually very effective—her clear, high voice balancing my deep, husky one. We did a sweeping tour of the front of the stage and finished the song together while moving offstage.

The curtain closed to thunderous applause.

☆ ☆ ☆

"Stupid, *stupid* shoes," Miranda hissed the second the curtain closed, dropping innocent, hopeful Dorothy like dirty clothes on the floor. "I told my mom they were slippery. It's *her* fault."

She glared at me. Hostile, as always.

"If you think this makes me your best friend, *Road*, forget it."

I couldn't help it.

I laughed.

Maybe I shouldn't have, because there's nothing as enraging as a person who laughs at you when you're mad, but the whole situation was so stupid and funny: Miranda standing there raging at me in her pretty Dorothy outfit, clutching her little basket with Toto the stuffie peeking out, me with my yellow face and Road costume. Teachers shaking glass out of my cape and sweeping frantically all around us.

All of it seemed so silly, somehow. So small.

It *was* small.

How had I ever let it get so big?

"News flash, Miranda," I said. "I don't want you to be my friend. I never did."

Miranda gave me a surprised look, then turned away.

And just like that, a weight lifted off me, and I knew I was free.

Madame Ducharme clattered and jangled onto the stage and swept me up in a tight hug.

"That was—" she searched for the right word "—*professional*, Diva. Like a pro!" It was clearly the highest compliment she could think of. "Bravo! The show, she must go on! People, people—ready for scene four!"

☆ ☆ ☆

No other mirrors were injured in the rest of the performance. It was strange: instead of being rattled by the accident, everybody seemed to step up. There was an unspoken feeling among the cast that we needed to pull together. And we did! We gave the best performance of the play we'd ever given. Miranda roared back from the accident, regaining her composure and throwing herself into her role. Kallie the Scarecrow actually remembered all her lines, Miko the Tin Man sang well, and Caleb the Lion got lots of laughs from the audience.

And I felt calm and relaxed. I was a presence. Not just any road—the Yellow Brick Road, the most iconic road in film history.

"And when you believe, when you truly believe you will get there, you will have arrived." I said my last line, before I turned and walked into the darkness at the back of the stage and the spotlights zeroed in on Dorothy and the others.

The Yellow Brick Road was finished, done. Not such a bad role after all.

"The end of the Road, Diva," Spencer said as he prepared to go onstage. "High five." Never has a high five felt so great.

I watched the last scenes from the wings. The assistants propping up the amazing, colorful backdrop for Emerald City. Dorothy throwing the water on the Wicked Witch of the West. Her cackly "I'm melting, *melting*" demise. Spencer, the Great and Powerful Oz revealed as just an odd and bumbling little man behind a curtain. I watched it all with a little smile on my face. It was good.

We were good.

Then the very last scene unfolded. The very last speech. The speech I'd practiced and practiced. The speech I butchered at first when I auditioned, the speech Madame Ducharme told me to repeat—Dorothy's "No place like home" speech. Miranda nailed it.

The curtain closed, and a roar went up from the audience.

The play was over.

Of course, this being St. George, it wasn't entirely over. The principal gave a little speech and Dorothy presented a bouquet of flowers to Madame Ducharme. Our director invited the cast out while the audience cheered and applauded again. It went on and on. Monkeys, then Munchkins, then the bigger roles: kids ran onstage and offstage while the audience clapped and clapped.

When she called for The Yellow Brick Road, I was surprised to hear the applause get louder as I swept out onto the stage.

I was even more surprised that I didn't feel like hiding.

I stood, with a smile on my face. This play had been so much work, especially considering I wasn't even sure I wanted to audition in the first place. Trying to figure out my weird part, then coping with Miranda's antics, then dreading rehearsal after rehearsal.

But I'd hoped to find a few friends, and I had.

I'd hoped to be a part of something, and I was.

I bowed, waved to my family, and stood back for the others to come onto the stage. Spencer got a big roar of applause when he came on. So did Miranda. They both deserved it. Then the whole cast joined hands (Spencer was on my right, someone else I can't remember on my left), raised them, then took a final bow.

Spencer turned to me with a big smile and gave my hand a final squeeze.

"Awesome!" he said.

That wonderful feeling that the dreams that you dare to dream really do come true.

★ ★ ★

"Deeeevaaa!" I heard my mom's voice before I saw my family weaving through the noisy crowd to congratulate me. Dad reached me first, sweeping me up in a hug, lifting me right off my feet.

"You did great," he said in my ear. "But no more plays. Please. My nerves can't stand it."

Then a massive bouquet of flowers launched itself at me. Mom was somewhere behind the flowers as she squashed them between us, throttle-hugged me, wiped away tears, and shrieked out congratulations all at the same time.

"Diva, you were divine! Magnificent! Awesome! Somebody,

quick, take a picture of my famous daughter and me!" She pulled me tight against her side.

As Dad pulled out his phone, I swept a fold of the Yellow Brick Road costume across Mom's shoulder like a scarf. She was tearful and my face paint was smeary, but in the picture, we were both relaxed and laughing and hugging.

"I think that's the nicest one we have of us," said Mom. "It's perfect!"

"Where's 'Ro?" I asked.

"He's back there somewhere—" Dad turned and gestured "—talking with one of his friends whose older sister was in the play. Oh, here he comes."

"Hey, Mom and Dad—" Hero's face was flushed with excitement "—can I go with Dylan's family to the Ice Creamery? Everybody's going there to celebrate." That was so perfect. It was my play, but Hero got the invite to the after-party.

I tapped him on the shoulder.

"Oh, hi, Deev. Hey, you didn't suck at all as the Yellow Brick Road. Not at all!"

"Stop. You're making me blush," I said sarcastically.

We were jostled by a crowd of Munchkins heading for the doors.

"Diva!" Shaya lifted both hands for high fives. "We did it! Great performance. And, more important, it's finally over! We're going to the Ice Creamery to celebrate! You coming?"

"See you there, Diva!" two other friends from my class, Catherine and Lila, called over their shoulders as they swept by with the rest of the crowd.

That counted as three invitations!

I turned, smiling, to my parents.

"Cast party? How glamorous!" my mom said excitedly. "Let's all go together! Don't worry. You can both hang out with your friends. We'll sit with the parents."

"And we're going to get you the biggest sundae on the menu," Dad said. "Whipped cream, cherries, the whole shebang."

We made our way to the door, stopping for the many people, some total strangers, who wanted to give me a high five, pat my back, or say "congratulations" or "great job." One parent said, "Well, Yellow Brick Road, you saved the whole show!"

Spencer and Jeremy sprinted past. Jeremy caught a glimpse of me over his shoulder.

"Diva! Ice Creamery!" he called.

"You gotta come, we need the Yellow Brick Road," Spencer yelled.

Five invites, but who's counting?

When we were finally at the door, I looked back into the almost empty theater. Madame Ducharme was onstage, talking animatedly to a small group of people. She caught my eye, smiled, and gave me two thumbs-up. High praise from her.

I smiled and waved back. It felt a little like I was

waving goodbye to the theater and the play, too. A happy wave. A thanks-for-everything wave.

I turned to go join my friends and eat some ice cream.

CHAPTER 22

No Place Like Home

S o, Mom, it's *your* birthday coming up next week," I said. "What should we do?"

She stopped what she was doing, which was glue-gunning flip-flops and fake tropical flowers onto vases for her upcoming beach-themed party, and tilted her head.

"You know what, Princess?" She gave me a strange look, then sighed. "I want you to throw me the kind of party *you* would have wanted for *your* birthday. Something simple, something small."

It was the closest we'd come to talking about *DIVAPALOOZA!*

That feeling of understanding each other without explanations, a long talk, or any words at all.

"That doesn't sound much like *you*, though," I said. "You always say that the party should fit the person, right? And you are definitely more of a hoopla party girl."

"Well, you know, what with all the parties I've done lately, and all the work for the play, I'm actually feeling a bit tired. A little partied out."

"Wow. *You*. Partied out. We should mark this on the calendar or something."

"I know, right?" She laughed. "Know what? I was going to surprise you with a cast party after the play—" she held up her hand as I flinched "—and then I thought that you probably wouldn't want that. So I didn't. See? I'm learning."

"Thanks, Mom. Sometimes it's more fun when a party happens spur-of-the-moment, with a few close friends. Like after the play, when we went for ice cream and then a bunch of friends went back to Spencer's house afterward."

"A pop-up party!" Mom said, nodding, lost in thought. "Totally spontaneous, spur-of-the-moment . . . I love the sound of that. Tucking that idea away for my business . . ."

I laughed. Mom would probably find a way to plan an incredibly detailed, elaborate, fake-spontaneous party.

"You know, Mom, you had a 'great feeling' about me being in the play, remember?" I remembered the sinking feeling I'd had at the time.

"I do!" She opened her eyes wide and clutched both hands over her heart. "I did! Right here!"

"Well, you were right. Thanks for giving me the little nudge I needed."

"So glad to hear it. Like, you have no idea how glad," Mom said. "I know Miranda was a real problem, hon. A few of the parents doing sets for the play told me she was a real stinker during rehearsals."

Somehow, the phrase "a real stinker" didn't quite capture the essence of Miranda's rude, toxic behavior, but I let that go. Her group left me alone, and I'd stopped worrying about them, or even noticing them. They seemed way smaller now.

"That girl is so—" Mom struggled to find words, then she snapped her fingers, pointed, and said triumphantly: "—insecure. That's what she is. Insecure."

I laughed. Again, a word that didn't really fit the complicated mess that was Miranda. Or did it?

I didn't know. And I wasn't really interested in finding out.

☆ ☆ ☆

I got Dad and Hero involved in planning Mom's party. We went out and found the perfect gift.

"Mom is gonna love this," Hero said, carefully holding the cardboard box on his lap on the way home. "Like, *LOVE* this." His face was flushed and excited.

It was a warm June evening. We strung multicolor lights inside the little gazebo in our backyard and spread a blanket on the floor. That evening, when Mom got back from the beach party, Hero had the job of bringing her outside.

"Did you see the balloons we tied around Gary the Centaur's head?" Hero's voice floated through the backyard as they came down the stairs.

"I did! He looked a*maz*ing! I wish I could figure out how to bring him to some of my parties. Maybe a mythical creatures theme . . ."

"Okay, now cover your eyes. Don't look!" I heard Hero tell her, and I saw Mom put her hand over her eyes.

Laughing and staggering, they lurched all the way through the enormous backyard. Dad lit the fire we'd built in the fire pit and flicked on some music from his phone. I set out the picnic dinner that Hero and I had made. We'd also bought a small cake and put a single candle on top.

And we'd hung a small sign that spelled out *MOM-MAPALOOZA!* in glittery letters.

☆ ☆ ☆

"Oh, it's so *magnificent* out here," sighed Mom as she finished her last bite of cake. "There's a beautiful pink glow from the house through the trees there. What a lovely, lovely party. All my favorite people, too."

"You still have to open your present!" said Hero.

"Yay, a present!" Mom said, sitting up.

"Yep, this is a fun one, Rosie," said Dad. "The kids spent a long time picking out something special for you. C'mon, into the house!"

"Oooh, mysterious," she said, struggling to her feet and excitedly trotting after us. "I just LOVE surprises!"

We led her to Hero's room, where we'd stored the present.

"Come in, come in, and *shut the door*," 'Ro said urgently.

Mom slammed the door quickly. "What? Why?"

"Because," he said, looking around his room, "because . . . be*cause* . . ." He got on his knees and looked under his bed. "Diva, where is he?"

"Here."

The kitten was hiding under a fold of blanket on 'Ro's bed.

"It's a real one this time, Mom." I held out the fuzzy little gray-and-white kitten. "Happy birthday!"

I think I can speak for Dad and 'Ro when I say that we were all totally, completely unprepared for Mom bursting into tears. Shock? Surprise? Delight? It was probably a mixture of all of those.

Dad slipped his arm around her.

"No, no, I *love* him," Mom sobbed, cuddling the kitten close. "It's just that he's such a gorgeous little thing, and this is just the best present ever, and I've always, always *wanted* a kitten, but it never seemed the right time."

"Well now you *got* one," 'Ro said. "And Diva picked the most special one at the Humane Society. There were lots of pushy kittens there that came right up to us, rubbing against us and purring. Lots of cuties. But *this* little guy was the only one who didn't. He looked scared and shy. Deev noticed him at the back. She said that all those other kittens would for sure be adopted, but this one actually *needed* us. He needed you. Says right on the certificate that he's shy and needs a lot of attention. His name is Bernie."

"Bernie," repeated Mom, wiping her nose. "Well, hello, gorgeous Bernie."

"You could change the name," I said. "You have a more . . . dramatic taste for names."

"I *like* Bernie," protested 'Ro.

"I kind of like it, too," said Dad.

Mom held the little kitten closer, burying her face in his soft fur.

"Mmm, well, there's nothing to say that his name couldn't be Bernard Octavius Pankowski III. Or something like that. Bernie for short. Oh, look, the little darling's fallen asleep. Still purring!"

Mom eased herself down on Hero's bed, lying with the cat nestled on her chest. Hero cuddled in. Then Dad lay down, too. Then me.

We lay there, all of us on the bed in the middle of Hero's ridiculous, circular room, listening to the faint thrum of Bernie purring.

"Wonderful birthday party, guys," murmured Mom, with her eyes closed. "The best."

That feeling of satisfaction where a phrase fits exactly what you're feeling just perfectly. In this case: "There's no place like home."

Acknowledgments

Thanks to my editor, Allison Cohen, for her keen eye and kindness, and to my agent, Hilary McMahon, for her generosity and support. I would also like to thank the entire team at Running Press Kids, Amber Morris, and Laura Horton for her wonderful illustrations.